Not All There

a NOVEL

Michelle A. Gabow

ISBN: 978-1-68471-159-8 (sc)
ISBN: 978-1-68471-161-1 (hc)
ISBN: 978-1-68471-160-4 (e)

Library of Congress Control Number: 2019918625

Lulu Publishing Services rev. date: 12/26/2019

To all those special friends who have chosen the road less traveled, who make life worth living, risks worth taking, and keep our souls alive.

Here is always beneath there.
—Mark Nepo

Contents

 She

I'm a very ordinary human being; I just
happen to like reading books.
—Haruki Murakami, *IQ84*

Preface to She and I

When I was married ... I suppose I still am. When I lived with Daniel, all I read was autobiographies—until I began to hate them. Maybe hate is too strong a word. Maybe it isn't. I was fascinated with how famous people lived their lives, managed to do whatever they wanted or deemed necessary, and talked about other famous people, as well as their unbiased perspectives on how they managed to achieve fame. Then one afternoon, the day after my birthday, strange occurrences took place in my life. A *friend* gave me a hideous journal for my birthday, which spiraled changes I could not have imagined. Strange books of fiction glided off bookshelves in front of me and opened to specific pages. Cafés popped up out of nowhere and disappeared as quickly. Strangers in restaurants, on the streets, in cabs, and in stores began revealing truths to me that were impossible to ignore—although I tried. I really did.

Suddenly I felt weary, or was it bored, with the famous, their need to leave their names engraved in our minds, their struggle with addictions, their fall, their rise, their friends, their films, their books, their loves without loving. I craved to enter the lives of so-called ordinary people who were rich with small things and moments. I gravitated toward books where the struggles of fictional characters validated mine, and their perceptions honored my own. I loved the joyful as well as the dreadful. I loved how these new (at least to me) novels kept things hidden and slowly opened. There was no rush, and I could read and breathe at the same time.

Reading was about living again. Real lives. My life began to welcome the mirror. To my surprise, there were infinite possibilities and not only in the books I began to read. Magic knew no boundaries. It lived behind, underneath, and in front of an ordinary life. It lived and breathed in each present moment. It cut a hole into the shape of the every day. But there are secrets to magic and secrets to seeing the magic. Every magician knows this. Some never tell. Some tell all, knowing only a few can hear.

This is my story. It makes no sense. It is the ravings of an old woman who will never be famous. So only a few of you may read this, which is fine by me. Because I know those few are supposed to find me, that being found is a mutual experience, and life presents itself if we let it.

So go on, open up, read. Take me to a park, to a café, preferably in Paris, by candlelight in the early morning, on your lunch breaks, on a bus going from one end of town to another. Lose me, find me again, bend, tear, mark me. Although I don't live for your caress, I invite it, because the heart is a wonderful place to dwell.

And whatever you do, try real hard not to make sense... of anything.

Chapter 1

The Gift

It's pale blue with little white sailboats. It makes her want to puke. Is this what Myrna thinks of her? Is she a pale-blue powder puff with little sails? "Who the fuck am I?" she utters louder than expected. She fingers the small padded material on the journal given to her by Myrna, her friend on occasion. Is this one of those occasions? She decides to make herself a pot of percolated coffee, her one holdout. Dan thinks it's ridiculous. Is it? Is she a ridiculous powder-blue puff? What the hell got her thinking this way? *This damn journal, that's what.* She should be at the gym and out for a good French red with the girls. That's where she should be. Myrna wasn't even going to be there. Jewel couldn't wait to have it slip out about her sometime friend's affair with Dr. Brockenberg, the dentist of the elite, knowing all too well that she was not the only one in this little group. It would be one of those minor slips, almost like a cough, a clearing of the throat, so to speak.

And yet, here she is. Percolating.

She sits at her kitchen counter, coffee in hand, and opens Myrna's damn journal.

December 17, 2015
My birthday. Happy birthday.

Be careful what you write. You never know who will find this and read all your personal fluff stuff. She laughs at her own joke. Or is she laughing because she is wondering why anyone would even be interested in her journal? She writes anyway.

> Planned a romantic night last night. Ordered fabulous food from Bistro Voltaire. Fabulous food but understated. Candles throughout. Wore my black off-the-shoulder Ralph Lauren. Cost a fortune. Worth a fortune. Arnold came to my home earlier that day. Worked out for two hours. Mostly Pilates. It takes work to have a body like this at thirty-eight. Hair blonder than ever in one of these new bob cuts. Can never tell if it's sexy or goofy. Hanna and Myrna and Pablo (the one and only hairdresser for years) say sexy. Everything is perfect. How lucky am I? Beautiful apartment overlooking the entire city and handsome cardiologist for a husband. Nobody ever wants to hear how good a life is. Perfection is just too painful for them.

She stops, has another cup of coffee, and sits as if frozen in time. She doesn't drink her coffee but has the cup in her hand, raised. Saluting her life. She is in her satin PJs. She is a statue of herself. There is really nothing more to say. She writes anyway.

> Forty-eight, okay. Forty-eight and looking not a day over thirty—or so everyone, including Dan, tells me.

Jewel walks over to the dining room mirror. It takes up almost a whole wall. Dan designed the apartment and bought that mirror. It really is a beauty. Gold leaf yet not gaudy. Dan told Jewel he bought it with her in mind—and added that he does everything with her in mind. "Now you can see yourself as I see you while you have your morning coffee." She plays with the curl on her bob, pulling it a few times so it is straight. She looks at herself for a second. She is a beautiful woman. A beautiful woman returns to the kitchen. Dan hates the kitchen, insists that every meal be taken in the dining room.

Last night's meal was in the dining room. Dan loved it, though he would have preferred to have dined at Bistro Voltaire. *His words.* "Why eat their food in when you can eat out? We're missing the ambience of the Bistro." He had a point. Don't know what I was thinking. We talked for hours about his patients. Always interesting stories. He told me several times how beautiful I looked last night. In the middle of a compliment, I asked Dan if he had ever been interested in other women. Dan's face turned red. "Interested in other women!" he gasped. Maybe that was the reaction I wanted. "What would make you think that? Other women can't compare to you. Who, Myrna? Hanna?" He burst out laughing. "Stupid women." I know this was the highest compliment, but women were always stupid—his nurses, the salespeople, even the waitresses at Bistro Voltaire. He always preferred a waiter. My friends, the newscasters, the bank tellers. All stupid. Except me, of course. Then Dan presented his gift. "Voila," he said. It was absolutely gorgeous. A diamond necklace. It lit up our dining room. I went to hug him, but instead he slipped on the necklace and clasped it in the back. Very sexy. Dan—he always knows the right thing to do. Though I have to admit I do prefer turquoise, my birthstone. I'm such a bitch. "Don't be a stupid woman," I said to myself, but it slid out. "Shit!" Again, out of my mouth. Dan, thank God, wasn't listening. I went to sleep in just my necklace, a little surprise for my man. Dan had some work to do but would join me. Did he?

Jewel closes her fluffy blue-and-white journal, walks over to the far right corner of the kitchen, and drops it in the trash bin.

***

Don't be mad once you see that he want it
If you liked it then you should've put a ring on it

Wuh uh oh uh uh oh oh uh oh uh uh oh
Wuh uh oh uh uh oh oh uh oh uh uh oh

Swish, swish, swish. She is fiercer than ever, fiercer than Beyoncé. She is not only burning fat on her stationary bike; she is burning period. Only a few more lyrics to go. She has it memorized. Then wine and salad with the girls, who are all here today. She has to skip the Myrna Mossip for another time, also Bistro Voltaire. Anything but Bistro Voltaire. But all the pedaling in the world will not appease her anger. Just looking back at Myrna sweating and mouthing the words makes her livid. Who the hell does she think she is? A puffy, white, middle-aged Beyoncé. Jewel laughs out loud at just the thought. Her day will come, and it can't be too soon. Just not today.

The girls decide on Caffé Opera for her birthday lunch. It is just down the street from the gym. She's actually up for their antipasto and wouldn't mind a few bottles of prosecco for the table. There are six of them today. Hannah makes a toast. "To Jewel, our dearest friend and our fearless leader."

They all laugh in unison. She supposes she is their leader. And then that fat pig, Myrna, adds, "To my best friend, the end of the thirties, and the beginning of a new era."

Jewel isn't sure if Myrna is going along with the joke or if she has lied to them so often it's what they all really think. Of course, it doesn't slip her mind that Myrna's joke might be on her. The girls raise their glasses and drink.

Myrna, who is seated next to her, the best friend and all, whispers, "Did you like my gift?"

"Oh," Jewel replies loudly for the whole table to hear, "I didn't open it yet, but I'm sure whatever it is, it is very tasteful and modern, coming from you. Of course, my best friends know my favorite colors."

Myrna sheepishly utters, as if taking dictation, "Red, black, and de—"

Jewel finishes her sentence. "And deep purple. There's nothing like a friend who really knows you."

There is an uncomfortable silence as Jewel sweetly watches Myrna squirm in her seat. Hannah breaks the silence by noticing Dan's necklace, which has them all immediately swooning. Dan is, after all, the perfect husband. This is what the perfect gift looks like; Jewel does not have to say it. However, when the group spots Carol across the room, the conversation shifts. She's newly divorced, has gained a ridiculous amount of weight, and is clearly wearing clothes off the rack. Carol always thought she was better than the rest of them because she was born into money. She is their topic of discussion and cause for much laughter for the entire lunch. And Jewel is more than relieved her birthday is no longer the main focus.

More than tipsy on her walk back to the parking lot, she decides not to go straight home like she told the girls. There is a little coffee bar / bookstore, not really her style, across the street from the gym. She enters, orders a café latte, and sits at a small table in the corner. However, she can't get that damn journal off her mind. Those little white sails in the middle of day-old pasta, leftover oatmeal, and stale bread. As she glances around the room, she notices a bunch of twenty- and thirtysomethings with their heads almost collapsed into their books or journals or sketchpads. They all think they have so much to say. Is she jealous? She drinks her coffee. At that age, she was not so different from them. A real nerd, Dan had said. Her friends were all outcasts, the few friends she had. She met Dan in a place like this. A young medical student. What he saw in her she'll never understand. She never fit in, and now look at her. He transformed her. She smiles at the thought. Suddenly, she becomes aware that there is a book on her café table.

She opens it somewhere in the middle, pretends to read, and then reads a line over and over: "She had made him possible. In that sense she was his God. Like God, she was neglected." Jewel closes the book and exits the coffee shop. When she is almost at the parking garage, she circles back, picks up *The Passion*, which is still lying facedown on the table, and places it in her Brahmin Hutchin satchel.

When she returns home, she finds herself rummaging through the trash now spread over the entire kitchen floor. *Where the hell is it?* When Jewel finally looks up, there is Dan, home from the hospital, staring in disbelief. She is sitting in the middle of trash with the filthy blue-and-white piece of fluff in her hands.

"What the fuck!" Dan shrieks.

Jewel hiccups and then has a fit of giggles, which quickly mutates into a strange over-the-top cackling. There was something unbearably funny about hearing this grown man shriek like a girl using *language,* especially since Dan takes considerable pride in the fact that he never uses *language*. Jewel hugs her journal in the middle of their garbage. The laughter continues until Dan bolts out of the kitchen.

This incident is never spoken about again.

Michelle A. Gabow

Chapter 2

Café Noir

Her knees ache from bicycling in place for what seems like hours. She is bicycling today to forget. However, she cannot for the life of her remember what she is trying to forget. A real conundrum. When the music stops, her body wilts, as if melting into the bike itself, and her mind shuts off. It is dead weight.

A gentle voice and a tap on the shoulder bring her back. *Back to where?*

"Are you okay?" whispers Hannah.

"Oh, I think I'm coming down with something." She's not lying. However, she has no idea what she is coming down with as she robotically walks with the girls to the locker room.

Jewel opens her locker and then is frozen. She glances inside as if she has never seen these clothes before. *Who do they belong to?* Right, they're hers of course. *Of course*. She wants to dress and dress quickly, no showering, no nothing, and leave. She is concentrating on moving her arm. It is not listening.

Myrna interrupts. "How about …"

Oh Jesus!

"… going to that new Thai restaurant to discuss the benefit dinner for the Children with HIV Foundation?"

For some odd reason, Jewel cannot speak. She is not able to make this simple decision. *To go or not to go?* This is not like her, not like her at all. *To go or not to go?* What kind of leader is this? She is still standing in front of her locker, unable to move. Just standing. Someone is playing a cruel joke. The soles of her Christian Louboutin sneakers are glued to the floor. Everyone in the locker room is staring at her. The girls are imitation cartoon characters with mouths agape.

Finally, "I really am coming down with something. I should go home."

They all nod and chirp. "Of course, you look pale, get some rest, we'll take care of things, I'll call …"

Jewel grabs her red wool Versace coat from her locker and begins to walk (more like sprint) before the sentence is completed. While rushing to get out of there, she spots Carol at a machine near the exit, smiles, pauses, touches her shoulder, and says goodbye. Carol broadly smiles back.

As Jewel closes the door behind her, she hears her own raised voice. "Why the fuck did I do that?"

She walks to the corner and then back again, opens the door to the same café and orders a latte and almond croissant. *Fuck the diet,* she doesn't say out loud. She grabs a book from the shelf without a clue to what she has chosen to accompany her latte and croissant. There is something old, familiar, and oddly gratifying about a book, any book. She is also acutely aware she is out of place here and the book is a much-needed security blanket.

A shadowy figure is standing next to her table. "Are you following me?" says an unfamiliar voice.

Jewel looks up in a stunned state, as if awakening from a dream. Carol is smiling. It takes Jewel a second to get the joke.

"I come here often but have never seen you. Is this your first time?"

Jewel answers simply, "No."

"Sorry to bother you. I'll let you get on with your reading." And then, "Murakami. You're a lady full of surprises."

"What's that supposed to mean?" Jewel replies with a significant sharpness to her tone.

"Oh, it's just that … I really meant it in a wonderful way. Honestly." Carol grabs the book off the table, turns to a page in the beginning, and reads. "'No one ever had a vivid impression of her face … Aomame resembled an insect skilled at biological mimicry. What she most wanted was to blend in the background by changing color and shape …' I used to feel like that."

Carol gently places the book back on the café table and walks over to the coffee bar to order. Jewel reads the quote over and over. Then she begins the book. How can a writer so effectively display this emotion with words, especially in regard to a character so different from her? There is something unfamiliar yet familiar about this book and her interaction with Carol. She silently sits for a while and looks over at Carol, who is engrossed in her own book. What is this emotion she is feeling? She sips more coffee and finishes her croissant. What is a word that could describe this feeling she is experiencing? Well, she is definitely no writer; that's for sure. Jewel walks over to the bar and pays for the book. She places it in her bag, slips on her coat, and exits.

While walking to the parking garage, the word grabs ahold of her along with a smile. "Intimate," she whispers to herself.

The same evening, Dan calls to tell her that he is working late. She can't contain her glee. Jewel does her happy dance, brings a bowl of Cheerios to her bedroom, lights a few candles, turns on the small light on the shelf of her bed, and opens Book 1 of *IQ84*. She has no awareness of time or anything around her for that matter. So, she is completely oblivious to Dan standing in the doorway.

"I'm home," he says sarcastically.

Jewel looks up at him, dazed.

"Are you reading or dreaming?" he asks.

Jewel doesn't speak, not because she can't. She truly does not have an answer to his question.

"It's midnight," he reminds her.

"Really … midnight … I was just getting to bed."

Dan tells her he will join her soon but has some work to do in the office.

She continues reading until the early hours of the morning. Tonight she knows for certain; Dan does not join her.

The digital clock blinks 5:00 a.m. Dan comes into the room, dressed and ready for work. He kisses her on the forehead while bringing her a cup of coffee and a glass of fresh orange juice on their silver Mizner breakfast tray.

"The perfect husband," she says, without a hint of sarcasm.

"I try." He smiles and sits on the corner of their bed.

"You look a little peaked this morning. Are you okay?"

Jewel nods her head yes but then adds, "Maybe I am coming down with something." It's become her favorite line this week.

"Perhaps you should see Pablo today. Your roots are coming in. Also don't forget, we're going to Opera Ball tonight. I picked out your dark blue Sophia Kah gown. You look beautiful in it."

"You're a rare breed, Dan, a cardiologist who knows his designers."

"You taught me well."

"Did I?" she utters flirtingly, uncovering a little more of her shoulders and chest from the quilt and even going as far as her sexiest come-hither flutter of the eyelashes.

He continues his line of thought. "Look your best because the Koch brothers will be there."

"Oh God. They're toxic. You know they gave hundreds of thousands of dollars to support the George Zimmerman Defense Fund and millions to the racist Tea Party. They are the racist Tea Party. You've always been a Democrat!" She detects a slightly hysterical tone to her words.

"I still am. They're powerful men who may give large sums to the hospital. And besides, they're working on their image."

"Just the fact that they have to work on their image should tell you something."

"Don't get all politically correct on me now. Feel better and please do something about your roots."

Dan throws a kiss from the bedroom doorway.

Roots. Something Dan and she had in common. The loss of their parents at a young age. It connected them in a profound way, their roots.

Jewel does not go to the gym, or answer phone calls, or make an appointment with Pablo. She lies in bed, gazing at the two moons on the cover of *IQ84*. Questions like bubbles pop up overhead, as if she is in her own animation. Pop … *Can this world really have two moons? Is there such thing as a parallel universe? Can a person live in two realities? Is seeing two moons in the night sky a form of mental illness? Is the protagonist insane?*

***

Before she realizes it, she is standing in front of the glass door to the café, glaring at her reflection in sweats, God help her. However, she at least had some wherewithal this morning to slip on her tweed Adidas sweat suit, which, truth be told, can be worn outside the gym. Jewel jiggles the door handle, but the door doesn't open. She spots the closed sign. Almost immediately, a hand turns it to open. A formidable, six-foot-tall woman appears in the doorway. Strong bodied, also in sweats, short gray Afro, oversized silver hoop earrings (out of place with the sweats), and bright red lipstick (also the antithesis of sweats). She is beautiful in a way Jewel is not accustomed to.

"The third time is the charm," the woman announces while walking over to the coffee bar.

How was this woman able to remember this was her third time at the café? How did Jewel not notice such a distinct proprietor?

Jewel follows her to the coffee bar.

"Café latte and an almond croissant, right?"

"Right."

"The name is Nancy."

"Nancy?"

"Yeah, I know. It doesn't quite fit. But it is my name."

"Jewel. Nice to meet you."

Nancy continues to brew the coffee and steam the milk.

"You're open kind of late for a café," Jewel voices.

"Oh no. We used to be open from ten at night until four in the morning. That's how it got its name, Café Noir. Just this week, we tried adding new hours, from two to five."

"That's why I never noticed the café before. It's odd hours, don't you think?"

"Mm, maybe. They're the in-between hours."

"In between what?"

"Normal café hours. Breakfast, lunch, dinner."

"Really. How's business?"

"Very good. Very good, indeed. You found us, didn't you?"

Jewel pays for her coffee and croissant.

"By the way, Carol won't be in today."

"How did you know ..."

"She's moved to Italy, a lifelong dream."

"Oh," is all Jewel can say, surprisingly sad at the loss of someone she barely knew.

Jewel slips off her St. Laurent classic leather jacket and pulls out her Murakami and her tomato-stained blue-and-white journal. She sips her latte but is unable to read or open her journal and returns it to its resting place in her bag. She keeps picturing Carol at an outdoor café in Florence, drinking cappuccino and having an animated conversation in Italian about the meaning of life with a male friend. The day is sunny. The streets are busy. And Carol is totally at ease in her new surroundings.

Jewel strolls to the bar to order another cup of coffee from Nancy and notices the café is suddenly packed.

"Wow, I didn't even hear anyone come in. It filled in lightning speed."

"Yes, it's like this sometimes. And other times, exceptionally empty. It was nearly empty the first afternoon you came here. I had a feeling it was a momentous occasion."

"My birthday."

"Ahh. We gave you Jeanette Winterson's *The Passion* for a gift."

"So sorry. I didn't realize I took the book until I reached my apartment." Jewel lies so easily it surprises her. Nancy probably saw her circle back and take it. Steal it.

"Oh no, no. The book was for the taking. Our customers often leave their favorite books on the table. It's a tradition at Café Noir."

While waiting, she is seized by a deep sorrow. *Is it Carol? How is that conversation about the meaning of life going?*

Nancy hands Jewel her latte, this time with a lovely froth on top and sprinkled with chocolate and cinnamon. More like a cappuccino. Jewel is back in Italy, sharing it now with Carol.

"Is something on your mind?" asks Nancy.

Jewel glances around the room. An odd bunch of characters, diverse in age, color, and, her guess, sexual preference. So unlike her gym right across the street. All with journals—writing, drawing, and reading. Not a laptop, iPad, or phone in sight. It's as if she has stepped into a different world.

"What is the meaning of all this?" questions Jewel.

"Of what? Café Noir? Life? Life …"

Jewel nods.

"Can't answer that for you. Café Noir is my answer." She hands Jewel her latte/cappuccino. As Jewel walks back to her café table, Nancy calls out after her, "I can tell you one thing though: the meaning of life is never static. It changes all the time. If it didn't, there would be no reason for our fabulous mistakes, would there?"

When Jewel returns to her table, she opens *IQ84* and reads, glances out the window, sips her coffee, and reads and sips and glances and reads. She reads the same passage over and over. And then over and over again. She pulls out her tomato-stained journal and a pen from her bag and writes down Murakami's words …

> "As some point in time, the world I knew either vanished or withdrew, and another world came into its place. Like the switching of a track. In other words, my mind, here and now, belongs to the world that was, but the world itself has already changed into something else … parallel worlds …"

"Two moons," she articulates out loud.

Jewel finishes her coffee, packs up her things, and exits Café Noir without even a wave goodbye to Nancy. It is pouring outside, an ice rain. Yet she does not go to the garage. She needs to walk. So she does, for hours. In the rainstorm.

Returning home in a shivering state with a temperature of 103, Jewel is unable to attend the ball. Her blue dress lies spread out on top of her quilt, with her under both. Dan is livid when he leaves, dressed to the nines, alone.

When she is sure he is gone, she yells with all her strength and delight, "And you can fuck the Koch brothers!"

Chapter 3

No Time

Jewel always had a certain amount of pride in how she managed time. Very well if she did say so herself, and she did say so herself. Often. She could manage the gym, social lunches, volunteer meetings, shopping, cooking, and phone calls while arranging Dan's social activities. Jewel liked being busy. She was proud of her schedule. It defined her. But things were changing. For weeks, she has not entered the gym. She has been leaving her home in her gym clothes, ready to take on the stationary bike, but turns right into the café every time. She doesn't answer phone calls, check her Facebook, or email a soul. She can't even relate what it is that she is doing. The closest word is nothing, which is odd, especially for her. Her relationship with Nancy is blossoming. Many times, Nancy joins her at her favorite table in the corner just to chat. Well, chatting isn't the right word. What is? To converse, to have a dialogue, to discuss without agenda, to think out loud together. Each day feels new. There is more to read, more to learn, more to touch.

For example, today. She wakes up and just sits in her bed. She is thinking about time. A smile brushes her lips. She asks herself, *How long is a minute?* She tests it. Without counting, she tries to guess when a minute is up. Several times, she seems sure of her answer.

But she is wrong. A minute is much longer than she ever imagined. A minute is a long time.

"Are you meditating?" echoes Dan's voice from the doorway. He is holding the silver tray with buttered toast, coffee, and fresh orange juice. What a husband he is!

She laughs awkwardly yet decides to tell him about her research on the minute. He looks at her stupefied. She quickly realizes this is the wrong person with whom to share her recent observations. She will wait until she visits with Nancy. Dan has a quizzical look. She supposes it is his way to show concern.

He sits on the bed and takes her hand in his. "Your friends are worried about you."

"Who?"

"Hannah, Myrna, Deana ..."

"They spoke to you?"

"Yes, they have been calling. You haven't returned their calls. They don't see you at the gym. You are not planning events. They can't contact you on Facebook. You are not returning their texts."

"Dan, I just ... I've been going to the café across the street from the gym."

"I told them that."

"Why didn't they just stop in Café Noir and see me if they are really concerned?"

"I told them that you have been going to this café across the street, but Myrna said that there is no café. The shades are always drawn where there was a café, and there is no sign."

"The café just has odd hours. Sometimes I think those girls can't see what's right in front of their noses. You said so yourself; maybe they are not very bright." Jewel does not feel good about the last sentence. She really doesn't want to corroborate his "women are stupid" diatribe at all, but she is a bit peeved at all of them. Then she adds, "I'm just doing a lot of reading these days. You always liked my intellect."

"That's not the point," he firmly pronounces, still holding her hand tightly.

"What is?"

"What is what?"

"The point."

"Have you looked in the mirror lately? You've let yourself go. You can barely see the blond in your hair anymore, and you are no longer the model-thin woman I married. I have a friend who is a great psychiatrist. Try to make an appointment today."

Dan hands Jewel his card, which she reads aloud. "Dr. Benjamin Barnes? That pompous asshole. You said so yourself."

"He's good at what he does. Call him today," he orders, then perfunctorily kisses her forehead and rises to leave. "Let me know when you set up an appointment."

She wants to rip the card into little pieces but instead looks in the mirror. Her hair is gray. She has put on quite a few pounds. Dan is right; she does not look like the Jewel of a month or so ago.

What exactly is letting yourself go? is her next research question.

She calls the doctor anyway from her bed. There is no denying something is happening to her. The appointment is made for next Thursday, the last week in February. Maybe she does need help. On the other hand, what can a psychiatrist really do for her except promote drugs or push for commitment? Dan and her friends would validate either treatment. A very, very scary thought. This may not be the answer. The debate drags her down. She grabs *IQ84* from her night table. Her valued anchor in the midst of a mind storm. It has developed into the Bible people keep by their bedside. However, a Bible may give solace, but it has never promoted change. The book opens up of its own free will to page 135.

> The everyday look of things might seem to change a little. Things may look different to you than they did before. But don't let appearances fool you. There is only one reality.

Perhaps she needs to consult with Nancy.

When Jewel is outside the café, she looks up for a sign for Café

Noir. There is none. The women were right. But the shades are up, and the café is bustling. As soon as she enters, Nancy brews her café latte. She doesn't have to order. She doesn't have to speak. How does Nancy know that is what she needs right now? Is she some kind of mind reader?

Her corner table is vacant. She makes herself comfortable, removes her coat, beret, and gloves, and extracts her Murakami, a fountain pen, and the stained journal from her bag. She wants to write. But what? How about a list—pros and cons of therapy with Dr. Benjamin Barnes.

Pros	Cons
Insight	Psychotropic drugs
Therapy	Committed to a mental hospital
Dan's happiness	Will that make me happy?
Return to my old way of life	Return to my old way of life
Physically fit and well put together	Loss of books
Active lifestyle	Loss of books and Nancy
Old friends	Loss of books, Café Noir, and Nancy
Repair good marriage	Repair marriage
Get back to myself	Myself?
Divorce	Divorce

Not helpful ... not helpful ... not helpful ...

Then Jewel's fountain pen begins to glide on its own accord on the lined paper inside her stained journal. Her hand is clearly attached but not moving it. It's like those old-fashioned Ouija boards. But it is not moving toward the "YES" or the "NO".

To begin again. Why is it so damn hard? It's as if it's someone else's story. It's my story, damn it. I begin with another cup of coffee. I begin with the rain tapping on my psyche. I begin in a soft, cloudy room with the sound of pens scratching paper. Soft café light, black-and-white photographs of writers I do not know on the walls, bright colored books still to read on the shelves, red tulips dancing in a paint jar on my table. "Ready?" they say. No, no, no, no, no, no. I begin anyway. Nancy keeps my cup fresh. I drink another cup of coffee and another and another— because I can, because this is what freedom, fuck you, love, persistence, karma, anger, obsession, breath looks like. It's like punching the air. It's not pretty or glamorous or volcanic. It's nonsense. Absolute nonsense. I am suddenly a fat, gray-haired, middle-aged woman. I begin anyway.

Her guided hand stops. The pen is still at the period at the end of "anyway." A smile parts her lips. She is frozen. Nothing moves. Even the café freezes. No one moves. Nancy is in the middle of a pour. The coffee rests in midair. Absolute stillness. She feels a lump in the back of her throat as if every uncried tear is sitting there. She coughs and starts to immediately choke. The room moves. Nancy is behind her, pressing her back. She falls to the floor. A strong man gives her the Heimlich. She twists and thrashes. Everything is turning. The café universe moves at incredible speed. Nancy and a few others are on the floor with her. Something pops, and the choked coughing ceases. Nancy and the strong young man help her to a chair. They are each holding a hand. She sees mouths moving but hears nothing.

Finally, Nancy's words enter. "Are you okay?"

Jewel shakes her head no. "I had a heart attack … I think."

"I'll call an ambulance."

"No, no. I'll be okay."

"Jewel, we shouldn't mess with things like this."

Jewel turns her journal page so Nancy can read it. Nancy looks up questioningly. The young man kisses her on the forehead and walks back to his café seat. Such a gentle gesture brings tears. Nancy and Jewel hold each other's hands in silence.

Nancy kisses Jewel's knuckles, looks again at the open journal, and whispers, "You did not have a heart attack but an attack of the heart."

"I remember..." Jewel states.

"What?" asks Nancy.

"I remember who I am."

Nancy kisses her on the forehead in the same manner as the young man and returns to her station. As she is walking, Jewel thinks she hears, "Ahh, then the café has done its magic." The entire café population applauds.

This occurs every now and then. The whole of the café breaks out in applause. A crazy bunch of characters. It kind of rises up in the café, usually after some sort of event that Jewel has no idea has taken place. However, something erupts in her, and she celebrates with them. In church, it would be called a halleluiah.

For the first time, Jewel is aware that she is the cause, the show of the day, but why is beyond her comprehension. She doesn't mind being the raison d'être if that is what she is. All she can think about now is Myrna. Did she give her the journal on purpose? Did she know consciously what she was doing? Or was it just a simple but unconscious birthday gift? Either way, she needs to call Myrna and genuinely thank her. Today.

Michelle A. Gabow

Chapter 4

The Obsession

Today never comes around. Instead, chatter takes its place in the form of tiny creatures pulling each ear to have their say.

Although it feels constant, it only happens at home. Café Noir represents that other moon, the other life, where these thoughts are just that. They come. Then they fade with a good passage from a book, or a smile from another patron, or the initial sip of her café au lait. Here is where Jewel can actually experience freedom from her own thoughts. The funny thing is she doesn't have to murder them or escape them. She just lets them in, and soon after, they find their own way to the door. A little like breathing. No, a lot like breathing.

Conversely, once she turns the key and walks into her apartment, these thoughts grab her neck, hang onto her chest, and babble incessantly in both ears. The words in her head, repeating over and over, are always a slightly altered parody of the same catchphrase of the same tune. They never really start in the beginning or have an end. They are ongoing, in progress, in the middle of a silent conversation persistently taking place in her head.

Well maybe ... Maybe Myrna wants me to write in the journal. Does she think there is something I need to know or learn or see that I wasn't? Is that a possibility? Possible but not probable. We're talking about Myrna.

Myrna! No, she probably went to one of those mainline stores, and of course this is the kind of crap they sell. But … but … what if there was more to Myrna than I thought? Maybe even more to Daniel? Who am I kidding? We're talking Myrna or Dan. Is it me? Have I grown into adulthood to become obtuse? Is that growth? Is that adulthood?

Stop!

And she does. She purposely stops. Thinks of that new Calvin Klein coat she saw in the *New York* magazine, the purple one with a flared skirt, almost like a tail. Imagines herself in that coat at an outdoor café in Florence for a casual lunch with Carol and a cappuccino. Sometimes Jewel sits, takes a moment, turns off the air, opens the living room window, and listens to the sounds of birds. Yes, the damn birds are out there in the world. Even in downtown Cleveland. And she stares out that window facing all those other windows in the high-rises across the street. Large windows. Never open. Shut tighter than tight. To keep Alfred Hitchcock's birds from flying in. Those damn birds attacking us, all of us in fear of their uprising. The real terrorists are just outside our very own very closed window.

Does Myrna know something I don't? Am I more clueless than Myrna? Can anyone be more clueless than Myrna? In all these years as being my pretend friend, was there a real friend living somewhere underneath? Who are my friends? Who are these people I've trusted but not really looked at all these years? Who is Dan? What world am I living in? Which moon?

The obsession, the questioning, the never-ending chatter occupies too many moments. Many of the questions are about Dan, questions she never gave voice to before. Not that they have a voice now. But they are here. They are frequent.

Jewel touches the arms of her chair. It is a cold, gray, unfamiliar chair. Where the hell is she? How did she get into this chair? This is the ultimate of lost. Is she dreaming? These occurrences, a kind of time travel, have become more frequent. Jewel finds herself in one place, and in what seems like seconds later, in another. She can't remember driving or walking there … here. But here she is. There is a rather ugly man sitting across from her. He is trying to be nice. She hates nice, especially now. Then she remembers. She wakes up. This is her appointment, the one she didn't really want to keep.

Suddenly tears. A goddamn flood.

Dr. Benjamin Barnes: "Why the sudden tears?"

Jewel shakes her head. She doesn't know. She is brain-dead. She never knows. Especially here in this cold, modern, very gray downtown office.

Dr. Benjamin Barnes: "Well, you were just talking about the journal with the sailboats …" He pauses and adds, "Again."

Jewel is furious but remains calm.

Dr. Benjamin Barnes: "Which led to Myrna, your best friend question mark, and then Dan."

Jewel is silent. She wants to be more interesting. But she is brain-dead. How the hell did she get here? Why can't she stop crying? There is no story to tell; her brain is empty. She wishes she had a good story, a fascinating reason for her tears. Sailboat Jewel, the most normal, boring woman in the world, had been prostituting each afternoon. In fact, she is now the Madame of Housewives Anonymous, a strictly upper-class house of call ladies of a certain age. Dr. Ben is, of course, the first person she has revealed this to. Or maybe the real truth is that aliens kidnapped her. They were from that other moon, the one nobody sees but Murakami's characters and perhaps Murakami himself. And suddenly she has a split brain and heart and is living in two worlds at once. In one, she is a famous novelist known for her gory but fascinating thrillers under the pseudonym of Bella Wright, and in the other, she has no memory …

Dr. Benjamin Barnes: "How is your relationship with your husband?"

Finally something Jewel knows the answer to. It comes out of her mouth like liquid gold, beautiful, clear, and well rehearsed.

Jewel: "Perfect. I met him at a very young age, in my last year of college, and he really did change my life." Pause. "About a month ago, he surprised me with a diamond necklace on my birthday. Dan entertains me every night with stories about his patients. Quite a lot of characters. I love listening to him. We rarely disagree. However,

Dan has noticed the changes in me and was the one who suggested I see you. He is truly concerned about my mental health."

The doctor is silent. Jewel is quite proud of herself.

Dr. Benjamin Barnes: "How is your sex life?"

Why do shrinks always go there? Fuck him and fuck Dan.

Jewel: "I suppose it's not high on either of our priority lists. He's busy. I'm crazy. At least lately."

Jewel likes that response. She sounds more interesting. She's crazy. Fuck yeah! She's something.

The doctor writes on what looks like a prescription pad, hands her the prescription, touches her hand, and plays with her fingers, perhaps a bit inappropriately. He massages her arm and holds her right hand in both of his in a strong grip. Then Dr. Ben gazes into her eyes.

Dr. Benjamin Barnes: "You are not crazy. You are suffering from midlife depression. Make an appointment with Sally, my receptionist, for later this week."

Jewel exits his office, stands in front of Sally for a few moments, tears up the prescription, sprinkles it over her desk, and heads for Café Noir, muttering to herself, "I am crazy, I am crazy..."

Jewel walks swiftly to Café Noir even though her gut rumbles as if she has just eaten bad clams. "Dr. Ben," she mumbles and giggles. As she gets closer, her pace quickens. She can't wait to talk to Nancy, her teacher of the unplanned, spirited conversation. Conversation is an art form at Café Noir, an art form Jewel has newly embraced.

Jewel arrives at the door out of breath, but it is locked. She pulls a few times before she notices the open sign is missing and there is no shade, drawn or otherwise. The tables, chairs, books, patrons, coffee machines, and Nancy have vanished. *Where? Why? Without warning? How could Nancy do this? Without telling me first?* They were friends. Real friends. Weren't they? Jewel turns her back to the door; she can't look inside. It is beyond contemplation. Her limp body slides down the cold glass to the cement pavement. *What just happened?*

The sun comes full circle. Jewel feels the sting of its rays. High heels, sneakers, boots scurry by. No one stops. No one asks if she is all right. She can see the gym across the street. Her gym. It seems miles away. The old Jewel returns to take care of the details. She helps the new Jewel up. While rising, she, the old and the new, notices the door sign to the cafe on the ground. The usual large black OPEN is facing her. However, underneath in small red-crayoned lettering are the words, "For you."

"For me?" Jewel questions loudly.

Behind the sign, still on the ground, is a package wrapped in plain brown paper. Jewel, the new Jewel, picks it up. Again in red crayon are large capital letters, "THAT MEANS YOU!" Jewel tears it open. Inside is a book by Jeanette Winterson, the first writer she read at Café Noir. It is entitled *Why Be Normal?*

Chapter 5

Tick

A month passes. Nothing changes.

Chapter 6

Tock ...

Months pass. Everything is back to normal. But not ... Her friends are in her life again. Pablo is coloring her hair. There is still that damn weight gain that she can't get rid of, especially around the gut. The time lapses are continuing with vehemence. Many times, Jewel is sitting in the middle of a restaurant, chatting with her friends, and has no idea how she got there. It's frightening, and she wishes she could talk about it. But the old Jewel does not speak of the new Jewel in public. Yet the old Jewel and the new Jewel are dying to express the life inside the Café Noir, the terrible loss they feel, the character of Nancy, and especially the books they are reading. The old Jewel is very controlling and knows when to keep her mouth shut. The new Jewel wants to scream. The old Jewel always wins in this argument that they allow themselves to have. However, the conversation sounds more and more like nails on a chalkboard to her. She believes that it's her penance for this reality, for which she is now grateful. The God's honest truth is that these girls have accepted Jewel back into the fold, readily and without apparent reservation.

Chapter 7

Ticket to Ride

Another month passes. Things change slightly. However, these changes make no sense to Jewel.

One Thursday morning, Jewel calls an Uber to pick her up. She texts the address of Café Noir as a destination, even though she is well aware that it is closed. A young woman pulls up outside her building in a Ford Focus. The woman calls out her name just to check, and she responds, "Are you Alberta?"

"Oui," says the olive-skinned young woman with wild, curly hair and a smile that warms the heart.

When Jewel steps into the car, she asserts, "I have a strange request."

"How fascinating."

Jewel is a little taken aback. The idea that anyone would even say that she is fascinating surprises and delights her. Also, Jewel loves the way she enunciates the word. *Faceeenateen.*

"Are you French?" Nothing like stating the obvious.

"Oui. Je suis originaire de Paris, mais mon mari est Américain. Nous vivons maintenant à Cleveland. Parlez-vous francais?"

"Non. Well … *un petit.* I always wanted to learn how to converse, but …"

"Qu'est ce que vous voulez, madame?"

"Is it possible that we could just drive around thirty dollars' worth to beautiful parts of the city?"

"Mmmm. Sorry you did not show up at the designated pickup. I will need to cancel service. You will be charged." She turns toward Jewel. "Il est possible."

"Merci. I'm happy with any decision you make."

"Okay."

They journey through the city of Cleveland. Jewel can't remember ever doing this before. Odd that this is the city she has been living in for more than thirty years and this is a first. The whole of the city comes back to life. The old and the new seem to fit like a well-designed puzzle. They pass Franklin Castle, Cleveland Arcade, the Public Square with the tallest skyscraper, Allen Memorial Library, Johnny's Little Bar … She remembers her and Dan in their better days sharing a burger and a beer. A tear crosses her cheek. Her eyes shut, and the softness of the breeze through the open windows washes her clean. The rest of the ride is spent with her eyes closed and her mind free.

"Je suis désolé, madame. Our thirty minutes are up."

Jewel awakens, not that she has been sleeping. Everything around her has this clarity, as if her world is now in HD.

"A bientot." Jewel remembers her French for *meet again soon.*

"Je ne pense pas."

A slap in the face. It is ridiculous she should even think they shared a moment.

Alberta continues, "It was enchanting meeting you. But I have a feeling that you won't be this way again."

Jewel stands by the driver's door, puzzled. What the hell would make her say that?

She surprisingly finds herself frantically knocking on the window of the driver's side of the Uber. Alberta rolls it down.

"You forgot *someting?*"

"Don't want to forget," Jewel replies. "Would you like to make a deal?"

Alberta smiles. "Sounds intriguing."

Chapter 8

A Forecast of Rain

Dan and Jewel are in the middle of a conversation. A conversation about what? Jewel isn't sure. Another one of her disappearances while in the midst of something. The space above her head tells her an ominous cloud dangles. There is no shelter. But the pressure is almost unbearable. It erupts. She is a wet mop, soaked to her core. She can no longer carry on. Silently, she breaks. Small droplets tap her brain, the window of her mind. The drops become larger. The tapping louder. It appears that she is profusely sweating. A hot flash of sorts. She is motionless and unable to form words.

"What does Dr. Barnes say about these lapses?"

Silence.

"These lapses?"

Silence.

"And the intense hot flashes …"

He noticed. "Sorry, what?"

"I asked …"

"Oh, the doctor. He says that we're making progress." (Lie.)

"It doesn't look like progress."

"No, it doesn't."

"Has Dr. Barnes prescribed medication?"

"Yes."

"Well, the important question is, are you taking it?"

"Yes." (Lie.)

"Do you mind if I discuss your meds with him? You know, doctor to doctor."

"No." (Lie.) *Of course I mind. I mind the whole damn thing. And you are not my fucking doctor!*

"Okay. I'll get right on it."

She can't even get thanks out of her mouth.

"There's another thing."

Oh shit.

"Ben told me to go easy with you regarding questions."

Oh, Ben did, did he? So you were already discussing my case.

"But ... I noticed that another car is in your parking space. Did you trade in your BMW for a Ford Focus? I just ... Jewel ... I just don't understand."

There is really nothing to say.

"Why, in God's name ..."

"Oh, Dan, it has nothing to do with God. I just didn't need the BMW. The Ford Focus is a newer model, and I made a small profit." (Lie.)

"Well, I hope the hell so."

Jewel hopes this is the end of the conversation and turns toward the bedroom, partially because now she realizes that Dan will not follow her inside. In a strange way, it has become her sanctuary, a room where she no longer has to lie ... about anything.

"Jewel, you loved that BMW!"

"Oh come on, Dan. It's just a car."

"Just a car? I want you to get the BMW back. I can't have my wife driving around in that car."

"Right. What would the neighbors think?"

"What would the neighbors think? Who are you?"

Dan is only a few steps behind her. A comfortable distance.

"Really," he reiterates. "Who are you?"

Jewel does not turn to answer. She opens her door. "I'm a damn Ford Focus. That's who."

And then she gently shuts the bedroom door behind her.

Chapter 9

Jewel's Chest

The next day ...

Jewel remains in her bed all morning, thinking about the Uber ride, her newly acquired Ford Focus, and that conversation with Dan. She is stuck in her bed and knows it is necessary to unstick herself. A stroll around the neighborhood is the perfect anecdote. Another first. She likes the idea of not having a destination. What do they call that in French? Oh yeah, *flaneur*, a person who walks the city in order to experience it. She slips on the striped shift that she usually wears around the house and a pair of sneaks, grabs her Roberto Cavalli bag and matching Cavalli kimono scarf for flair, and rushes out the door. Is it locked? Not bothering to check, she enters the elevator.

The only way to release herself before she tumbles into the world of obsession is to put one foot in front of the other. *Just one foot in front of the other.*

As soon as she walks out the glass door of her apartment building, two seemingly disparate things strike her, a miniature, cherry, French, provincial bureau on the curb and a splendidly tall man. He is at least 6'7" with a sense of perfect style that takes her aback. He entertains a Moroccan scarf, casual suede jacket, straw fedora, and deep purple, linen pants. She wants to rush upstairs and change but just stares, a little dumbfounded.

He smiles. "I mean really. Do you believe this is sitting right here on the curb? Fabu, right?"

"Yes, it is." Jewel moves closer and touches it. Smooth cherry wood, an antique in flawless condition.

"Do you want it? I just have too much stuff that I haven't even started to unpack. So sorry. The name is Frederick. Just moved in. You must have it. I'll take it upstairs."

"Well, I do have some room next to my bed."

"And you are?"

"Jewel."

"How perfect. A jewelry box for a jewel."

The small bureau is ridiculously heavy and needs both of them to bring it to the elevator. They struggle and grunt and laugh all the way up. They place it in the middle of the living room so they can admire it from all angles.

"Oh damn, where are my manners? Would you like something to drink?"

"Oh, I just love the fact that you have them."

"What?"

"Manners, my dear. Manners. So rare these days."

"Coffee or tea?"

"Chardonnay, if you have?"

Jewel wants to say, "But it's ten o'clock in the morning," yet controls the urge. As she pulls out Dan's most expensive bottle, a smile takes hold.

From the living room, she hears a scream of delight and then, "Come in quick!"

All the drawers of the bureau are open, even the side doors. Jewel is astonished for a moment that it even has side doors.

"Amazing!" she exclaims.

"No, that isn't even the amazing part."

As Jewel moves closer, wine bottle and glasses in hand, she notices that all the jewelry is still in the bureau, hanging off of hooks inside the open doors, filling the drawers.

"Do you think it's someone's mistake?" she asks.

"No … I kept checking. It's been out there since early last night. A bottle of Montrachet. Oh, I think I'm in love!"

"My husband knows his wines."

"Before partaking, I need to stop at the little boy's room. In what direction?"

She tells him, and as he passes the dining room mirror, he pronounces, "Fabulous. Are you sure you're not a gay man?"

"Dan, my husband, picked out the mirror as well as some of my designer clothes."

"Interesting."

When Frederick returns, wine already poured by Jewel, he says, "And the Cavalli kimono scarf?"

"My decision," she states proudly.

"Of course. Let's trade for now." Frederick wraps his Moroccan scarf around her neck, and she does the same. They toast and drink. He holds the wine and swirls it in the glass. "Let's savor this moment of wine and meeting."

"Yes."

"Because I have learned too well that these are the moments that make a life."

They finish one bottle and begin another. Frederick orders Indian takeout from a restaurant he knows that is located near his shop. He tells Jewel about his lover, the love of his life, who recently passed. He cries. Jewel holds him. Between tears, Frederick tells stories about Gays in the Millinery, their shop downtown where new and used scarves and hats are sold on consignment. "Just up your alley," he says.

There is something about these stories that reminds her of Dan, the Dan she remembers loving. They're character driven and charming. Like Dan, his gestures are slightly over the top, which makes them funnier and more real at the same time.

The food is delivered, *saag* paneer, vegetable *pakoora*, *chana* masala, tandoori chicken, naan, paratha and *ras malai*. A feast. They eat, drink, laugh, and try on jewelry.

The jewelry in the chest is nothing like her own. Daintiness is out of the question. There are no diamonds. Instead, it is filled with numerous pieces with stones of turquoise; amethyst; carnelian; bloodstone; black pearls; handcrafted silver; large, artsy, hanging earrings; cuffs; and an age-old Indian silver necklace with garnets. They are from another life, perhaps more like Frederick's. Jewel carefully places a hanging, copper, basket weave earring on Frederick's left ear. He in turn gently arranges an Indian necklace and large, black, wire hoop earrings (more like bracelets) on her. They slide cuffs and bracelets down both arms, completely covering their forearms. Wrapped around their necks are strands of black pearls, enough for both of them.

Jewel brings in her makeup, and they creatively design their faces, giggling and drinking the whole time. She is acutely aware that she is trying on a new life, or is it an old life? "What the fuck," she whispers as they clink their wine glasses.

While Frederick dresses several times, Jewel gets a pair of scissors from her kitchen.

"How are your barbering skills?" she inquires.

"Excellent."

"Cut."

"How short?"

"Very."

Her bob quickly disappears. The *c* curls and strands of bottled Blissful Blonde are strewn across the dining room floor. All that remains is a bizarre pixie haircut and her roots.

Chapter 10

Oh Shit!

"Oh my God," Pablo keeps repeating like a broken record when she slips off the scarf that shielded her chopped coiffure from Dan all of the evening and early-morning hours. Of course Dan noticed.

"I'm testing out a new product that claims to keep hair shiny all day." Lying was too damn easy. But her afternoon with Frederick was difficult to explain, especially to Dan, or any of her friends for that matter.

With Pablo, she simply says, "Don't ask. Can you do something?"

While Pablo works his magic, Myrna enters the salon.

"Oh shit," Jewel exclaims more audibly than intended.

Pablo keeps working; however, Jewel is certain that this line along with his own brand of narrative of her exchange with Myrna will be repeated several times during the salon hours.

"Your hair!" Myrna blurts out. And then surprisingly, "I kind of like it."

Jewel smiles. "I do too."

Pablo announces that he is amazing. Jewel has to admit that he has done his magic.

"Are you going to color it?"

Instantly and simultaneously, Pablo responds with a yes, and Jewel with a no.

Myrna laughs and adds, "I love that you always know your own mind."

"Do I?"

A distinct hush brushes between Myrna and Jewel. There is something uncanny about it. Right. Myrna is not talking. When she finally speaks, Myrna doesn't break the uncomfortable silence. Her following words grow out of it.

"Are you writing in your journal?"

Pause.

"I bought a similar journal for myself the same day I bought yours. I knew it wasn't your style, but … I write in mine every day."

"You do?"

"Yeah … It's the best me, the most honest me, the scared-as-shitless me, the me I hide from the world, even my friends. I don't know what I was thinking. I guess … maybe for some reason it would bring us closer."

Something in Jewel's heart shifts. She can't explain it. But everything, even Myrna, especially Myrna, softens.

"Thank you."

Chapter 11

The Bow

Jewel is very lucky in her privileged way. She doesn't have to work. Dan provides a good life for her. Her younger self, the self before Dan, the unsure self, the poor self, the searching self, the self who had a partial scholarship and three jobs to put her through school, the self who secretly wrote poetry in her dorm closet, who relished her nerdy friends, the dreamer, the self who grew up in halfway houses (orphanages by another name), the self who always had to struggle ... she is gone. In her place is a rich, busy woman who volunteers and organizes and gossips. She has never really known if she likes or dislikes this woman. She was just so happy to finally be her. Now, she's a prisoner of her own rebellion. Or maybe she was always a prisoner, clutching to the bars that held her. A stunningly thin— emphasize thin—upper-class leader, with beautiful blond hair and designer clothes, disguised and imprisoned by her own manufactured self-worth.

This morning in bed, Jewel reads three lines over and over in her newly found novel. What is amazing is someone else already highlighted them. They are in bright pink and popped up just like the book did. In fact, this morning, the page turned to them without her help.

In the middle of the night, some months later, holding her own heart, feeling nothing, Anna had looked at herself in the bathroom. There she was. It was the there-she-was guise.

This novel, these words, found her yesterday while she was on a search for Frederick. She wouldn't let him slip through her life like Nancy. But she wasn't having much luck. First she talked to the custodian, then the doorman to her building. Neither of them remembered a six-foot-seven African American tenant. "Really?" she kept saying. He was that unforgettable. The doorman was there when they discovered the jewelry chest. He still had no recollection. She called the management, who insisted there had been no new tenants in the last four months. Jewel kept maintaining that Frederick left his beautiful Moroccan scarf in her condo, and she wanted to return it. However, the unbelievably uptight woman on the phone kept asking for Frederick's last name, which of course Jewel never got a hold of.

"You should expect a call from my husband, Dr. Daniel Goldman, tomorrow," Jewel announced and immediately hung up.

She and Dan had lived in this friggin' building for over fourteen years and never asked for one goddamn favor. Leaving the apartment complex in a huff, Jewel was determined. It was the day after her interaction with Myrna, and she desperately needed to share the experience with Frederick. Something was changing in her, and there was a strong desire to reveal this shift in her perspective to someone she trusted to understand. Jewel discovered an old phonebook from 2012 and looked up Gays in the Millinery. She found it off Detroit Avenue and was out the door. The doorman said hello, but all she could do was deliver the fuck finger, not that he could see it from the back of her.

Jewel's pace was quick, and every now and then, *language* would escape from her mouth. Some strangers would glare, some would ignore, and others would smile. For the first time in her adult life, she didn't give a shit. Jewel was on a mission.

A mission to keep her new friend. A mission to talk about what was really on her mind. Then suddenly, wham! A book jumped out of an outdoor bookcase. Jumped! She tripped and had a hard time regaining her balance. This definitely put a cramp on her style and her pace. She wanted to pick up that book and throw it into the window of the bookstore it was attached to. Grabbing it, Jewel walked inside, ready to give the owner a piece of her now-very-important mind.

"This book jumped off the bookshelf, and ..." She was startlingly aware of how ridiculous she sounded and couldn't help but notice this beautiful male relic of the sixties with such a grin on his face that his long gray beard seemed to part like the sea.

"Ahh." He beamed. "The unfinished title."

Jewel read the title, *There But For The*, by Ali Smith. Then out of her mouth that obviously left its filter at home came, "If I didn't know better, I could swear that Nancy put a spell on me."

"Nancy put a spell on all of us," the storeowner exclaimed.

Jewel couldn't believe her ears. "You know Nancy!"

"Well, of course. Café Noir, right?"

"Yes ... *yes!*" After taking a few seconds to digest, she asked, "Where is Nancy? And what the hell is her last name?"

"Oh. You're a Café Noir person. I meet so few these days."

Jewel didn't know where this man went next, but he unquestionably was not there in the store.

"Hello? Anybody home?" That was most definitely a remark of her old self busting through.

"Sorry. Sometimes memories take me away. I kind of like where I go. I used to take drugs. Now, just a line from a book, a swing of the front door, or a question can get me there. Who knew I could get high without the use of illicit drugs? Or maybe I practiced so hard when I was young I can now manage to create this state naturally. Pretty damn cool, huh?"

Jewel couldn't help but smile.

"Nancy, huh? Fuckin' fantastic Nancy. We had a little thing goin' at one time. But the truth is all the independent bookstores know each other; it's a sadly small community. But growing. Growing all the time. You know those pop-up restaurants that are showing up all over the country?" He didn't wait for any recognition. "Well, our Nancy had this idea of pop-up used bookstores. Many times in abandoned buildings or ones with really cheap rents. They would pop; special people would find them, and then they'd disappear. Nah ... I don't know where Nancy is. I know that she is no longer in Cleveland. And no, I don't know her last name. I'm not even sure if her first name is Nancy. In Hebrew, the meaning of Nancy is *grace*. I'm sure of that."

"What is it with you people and no last names?"

"Oh, that's a long story. And you really had to be a radical in the sixties to understand it."

"Well, my name is Jewel. Jewel Goldman."

"For you, my dear, Jerry Schwartz and the book is my gift to *The Jewel*."

"No, I can't. Really, I have the money."

"Oh no. It is fuckin' crucial, my dear, that I give this to you. Because I'm sure, like you are, Nancy put her spell on you."

"I'll be back."

"I hope so, my dear. But if not ... continue."

"Continue what?"

"Your adventure."

Jewel continued, wondering how the hell these people make a living. Before she knew it, she was walking down Detroit Avenue and then making a left on Sixty-Ninth. She looked up, and there it was! The rusty and barely visible sign was so weathered it surprised her. Nevertheless, it read Gays in the Millinery. She could hardly contain her anticipation as she sprinted through the door. Behind the counter was an Indian woman, perhaps Hindu, wearing a magnificent sari with shades of purple, blue, and soft reds that gave the impression of watercolors dancing with every move. Her lengthy silk scarf complemented all the hues of the sari but exhibited no separation between each color. Both the oneness and diversity of color was so spectacular that Jewel actually had to take a breath.

"Sorry," Jewel apologized. "It's your scarf. So ..."

"I know ... it is breathtaking. A very dear friend gave this to me."

"Could that friend be Frederick?"

"Yes, yes!" The saleswoman rushed around the counter in tears and hugged Jewel. "You are a friend of Frederick also?" She withdrew almost as quickly. "I'm so sorry. It is not like me to be this demonstrative with my affections."

"I get it. Frederick is amazing. Is he here today?"

The woman's manner went through a 360-degree change in a matter of seconds. "How exactly do you know Frederick?"

"I met him last week outside my apartment building. He had just moved in, although nobody can seem to remember him. We were both ogling a small 1950's jewelry chest."

"Really," the woman said suspiciously.

"Yes, Frederick, the six-foot-seven African American with a Moroccan scarf who owns this store. Just ask him. He'll tell you."

"Sorry. I cannot honor your request because …"

The saleswoman returned to behind the counter and leaned on it as if that was the only way she could still stand.

"Frederick passed two weeks ago."

"That's impossible. You're thinking of his lover. He was heartbroken."

"I don't know who you are, but I think you should leave. Now!"

"Wait." Jewel pulled out the Moroccan scarf from her bag. "I was returning it."

The woman held it to her nostrils and inhaled. "Patchouli and amber."

"See. There is some mistake. I was with him, clear as day. He came up to my apartment. We drank his favorite white wine, a bottle of Montrachet. We laughed so hard I almost peed in my pants. We creatively applied makeup to each other's faces. For God's sake, I let him cut my damn hair." Jewel pointed to her now very short pixie.

The lady seemed fixated on the scarf. "Where did you get this? Where?"

This woman seemed certifiable to Jewel, and she decided this in fact would be as good a time as any to exit. As she was about to leave, she shouted, "When Frederick returns, let him know I was here."

"Returns?"

"Yes, returns from the dead," Jewel answered sarcastically.

"Oh my God!" the woman exclaimed. "Stop!"

Every bone in Jewel's body wanted to go, but she stood at the door, frozen. She heard a key turn and a drawer open and close. Before she knew it, the saleswoman was right behind her. Probably with a gun. The woman asked her to turn around. "Look, look," she said. Jewel cautiously turned. The lady passed her a piece of notarized something. "It's the deed to the building and store. He left it for me before he took his life."

She read it. It was. "You're asking me to believe … Frederick killed himself?" She felt a stabbing pain in her heart and had trouble catching her breath. "How could that be?"

"He was not the same man after Jonathan died. It was not the same life for him."

"What the hell are you saying?"

"I'm saying our Frederick paid you a visit. I don't know why it was you."

"A visit?"

"Yes, you had a visitor."

"These things just don't happen in my world."

"Perhaps your world is changing." The storeowner gently placed her silk scarf around Jewel's neck.

"I can't take this."

"Frederick knew of your love of scarves. That is so, yes?"

"Well …"

"Please. It's the least I could do for my rude behavior. It has been an odd meeting, to say the very least. But I know you are supposed to wear this. Deep in my soul … And you do also."

The woman clasped her hands together, fingers pointing upward as if in prayer, and bowed. Jewel reciprocated with a bow. Something happened in that moment, a kind of release of the heart. What is humility but that release? Jewel silently vowed she would explore the bow more often.

Dizzy from all this, she readied herself to leave but had to ask one more question. "I'd like to know your name."

"Amita," replied the friend of Frederick.

Jewel wanted to ask what it meant but didn't.

"Without limits," Amita replied to the unasked question and smiled.

****

It's morning. Jewel is still in bed reading the line from the book *There But For The*, over and over again. It was already underlined in hot pink marker. Perhaps by the last reader. Perhaps by Nancy.

> There were several reasons at that particular time in
> Anna Hardie's life for her wondering what it meant,
> herself, to be there …

Jewel feels more unsure of everything than ever before. This whole visitor thing has disturbed her to the core. She would like to knock it up as just plain crazy. But if she is to be honest, she has had these visits before. Before Dan. She remembers her mother, who had died many years before, walking into her dorm room. As plain as day. She was wearing her red button-down sweater and looking for something. She remembers calling to her and her mom appearing confused. Another memory/visit took place while she was taking her final exams in college. Jewel looked up from her paper and saw her mother in the door window to the room. Again, she was in her red cardigan. Her mother was staring in the window, hand above her eyes, searching. "Here I am!" Jewel wanted to scream. But her mom stared at her blankly and walked away. The memory of the shock of that still feels tender and real.

Jewel gently rises from her comfortable bed, strolls into her dining room, and stands for a few moments. It looks as if she is in a sleepwalking state, but she has never felt more awake. She bows to Frederick as if beginning their dance, bows to Nancy for the hot pink marker, bows to Myrna for the blue-and-white sailboats, and promises Jerry Schwartz to continue. She wraps Amita's silk scarf around her neck several times and stares at her naked body in the dining room mirror.

> There were several reasons at that particular time
> in [Jewel Goldman's] life for her wondering what it
> meant, herself, to be there ...

Chapter 12

A Tall Tale?

Jewel made a conscious effort to have a real conversation with Daniel about her new acquaintances, which were far deeper than any of her so-called friends. She wanted to believe that Dan could listen, because Dan was her life as she knew it.

He came home, as usual, very late on Thursday evening. Jewel had a bottle of Courvoisier on the dining room table with two glass tumblers already poured. When he saw her, he smiled. "You waited up for me."

The truth of that statement flashed before her. Her role in the breakdown of the marriage stunned and saddened her. Even more reason to talk. She thought she would start with a simple question.

"How was your day?" To the point. No need to jump into her day. Not yet.

Dan began his monologue of stories about his patients. She always loved the flamboyance and vitality of his style. Today she noticed something else. She had observed it before but paid it no mind. It became especially apparent to her during her time with Frederick. Their storytelling was remarkably similar. As Dan progressed, his gestures, the sound of his voice, and the lilt of his words were almost effeminate. It was as if he was hiding behind a certain masculinity that disappeared as the story became alive.

She was listening or maybe pretend listening. It was one of his longer monologues. She didn't remember when the actual stories began a shift. However, she was more than slightly aware that a shift did happen.

"I can't believe how attuned he is to what I need during surgery. Actually, now he studies some of the x-rays with me. I am amazed at his interpretation, how well he reads them. I don't know why he chose to be a nurse rather than a doctor." Then Daniel gushed, "We have the most fascinating conversations about the patients. I don't care if they say it's sexist or not, a male nurse is so much more capable than all of my female nurses put together."

"Really," was all she could manage to say.

"Yes, really."

"Dan, you seem quite taken with … what's his name?"

"I'm not quite taken with him. He's just good at his job. Jesus, Jewel, does everything have to have a sexual connotation?"

"Who said anything about sex?"

Now he was angry. Oh God, this took a downhill turn pretty quickly. And she hadn't even mentioned Frederick, whom she so wanted to talk about. "Sorry, Dan. I really didn't mean anything by it. What is his name?" But really she wanted to scream at him. *You are such a defensive, sexist asshole.*

"Martin." He literally clenched his jaw tight, which made for an uncomfortable silence. Then his whole body switched. His machismo returned full fledge. He was actually flexing his new muscles.

When did Dan get such protruding and defined muscles?

"Enough about me. How was your week?" he asked abruptly.

She was so shocked that she didn't notice the lack of kindness in his voice. Only the question stood out. How was *your* week? *This is it! This is the time! Forget about Martin,* she thought, but something nagged at her. What was it about his new nurse that disturbed her? Was she jealous? She took a long swig of her Courvoisier and poured another.

"You want to hear about my week?"

"Well, I asked, didn't I?"

Jewel jumped into her story with exuberance. She had a story to tell. An interesting story. Her own story. She began with the jewelry chest, the first sight of it and of course the first sight of Frederick. She loved the details of what Frederick was wearing and their sporadic laughter as they dragged the heavy chest to the elevator. She described their time together, the wine in the afternoon, how Frederick admired the dining room mirror, and all the fabulous jewelry still left in the chest. There was no need to upset Daniel, so she left out of her detailed description the label of the bottle of wine and another very important element of the tale, Frederick's visit from the dead. She was still trying to get around that one herself. When she was through, she was exhilarated and out of breath. For the first time, Jewel understood the power and pleasure of telling a story. She truly understood Dan!

Dan stared at her in silence. There was no smile on his face, but there wasn't a frown either.

"So, let me get this straight. You picked up a homeless black man from the streets—"

"Dan, Frederick isn't homeless. He lives in this apartment complex."

"Really. Which apartment?"

"I'm ..."

"Right. You shared a bottle of wine ... Oh my God, I hope it wasn't the Montrachet. Shit! It was a hundred-dollar bottle of wine. Are you out of your mind? You could have been raped or killed."

Jewel wasn't sure if Dan was more upset about the Montrachet or the possible rape of his wife.

"I used to think you were smarter than most of the women friends in your so-called group. Now I just don't know what to think. More to the point, what the fuck are you thinking? What the hell are you doing with your life?"

"What the hell are you doing with yours?"

"Really," snickered Dan. "That's your comeback. I'm going to my office."

He shut his office door. Jewel poured herself another shot and then another and then ...

What the hell are you doing with your life? She couldn't believe she asked him that.

He's a cardiologist, for God's sake. Suddenly she saw herself through Dan's eyes. Bringing home a stranger. Actually, a dead stranger, to be quite frank. Her tale was not about wacky patients but about her own bizarre behavior.

How crazy am I?

Michelle A. Gabow

Chapter 13

Can Beggars Be Choosers?

It's morning ...

Jewel raises her head from the dining room table, where she apparently slept. Her head aches, and her stomach feels more than queasy. She glances at her watch. Eleven o'clock. Dan, of course, is already at the hospital. He must have seen her with her head like a rock on the table and just left her there. She enters the kitchen. Coffee has been made on Daniel's ultramodern espresso machine. She pours a cup into a demitasse and drinks. Not her favorite. She much prefers her old-fashioned percolator. But beggars can't be choosers. She reviews the evening in her head, walks to the bedroom, cup still in hand, and removes the stained sailboat journal from her night table drawer. Balancing both cup and journal all the way to the kitchen table, Jewel sets them before her, opens the journal to a blank page, and writes:

> It's morning ...
> Late, late, late morning. I awake from the nightmare called my life. What is happening to my marriage? When did Dan begin to hate women? When did I begin to behave like a mad woman? Am I crazy? Is he? I remember early in the marriage how Daniel

preferred to talk in a room of women rather than hang out with the men. He was much more interested in décor and style than sports. I loved that about him. He wasn't like other men. All my friends confided crushes on him. Who could blame them? I had the perfect husband. When did that change? Was it before the journal? How long have I been walking around only half here? Who the hell am I anyway? I was happy? Or content? Or blind? I don't mind being blind? Fuck blue-and-white sailboats, Murakami, Café Noir, Nancy? Fuck it all! I don't want to wake up or have my best times with a dead man. Holy shit! I can't write another damn word. Done. I'm done. There's no more to say.

Jewel walks to her bedroom, returns the blue-and-white sailboats to her drawer, lies down into her silk bed sheets, and falls sound asleep for two days. No one wakes her. She finally rises, takes a shower, and dresses in her Calvin jeans and a T-shirt. It's six thirty in the evening. She watches herself pour the box of Cheerios into her largest salad bowl, as if a witness. But to what? She gobbles the Cheerios down as if it is her last meal. The Os can't be shoved in her mouth fast enough. Cheerios fall to the floor, raining from her lips. Well, if it is her last meal, it will be her favorite. And isn't that what a last meal always is? A totally full zombie enters the living room and puts on the seven o'clock news. The television, as large as the wall itself, lights up and mesmerizes her for a few moments. She hears the word suicide but is not sure if it's coming from the TV or the voice in her head. *Suicide . . .*

Out of nowhere, there is a pat on her head. Dan does not say, "Good dog." Instead, he kisses her on the forehead. *What?* He loosens his tie, goes to the kitchen, brings in two glasses of red wine, and sits on the chair next to Jewel's. They watch the nightly news. He talks back to the television with his own explanation and narrative. It is every night of their marriage.

Chapter 14

Word!

Jewel tries to think of the right word that captures what she's experiencing at this very moment. Disconnected? Despondent? Maybe. Hopeless? Yes, that too. She imagines her life as a novel. What would be the title? *The Homeless Housewife. Maladjusted Moon. Hallmark Hell. Dead Man Talking.* A smile parts her lips. Words have taken on a profound significance. The beauty of language to lay bare the truth of a life has changed Jewel. However, Jewel doesn't want to change. That duality is driving her slightly, maybe not so slightly, mad.

Can the old Jewel and the new Jewel exist as one?

Jewel finds *1Q84*. *Damn you and your two moons!* She turns to page 135, as if her hands have been instructed to by some outside force, opens up the sailboats to an empty page, and writes down Murakami's words (already underlined): "Things may look different to you than they did before. But don't let appearances fool you. There is only one reality."

What the hell does that mean?

Chapter 15

A Simple Note

It is late afternoon. Even the sun whispers ... *You have to have a plan.* Daniel's favorite and most often articulated pronouncement. It seems like he knew. He has obtained all of life's dreams—a profession as a cardiologist (well-known, well respected, and well paid), a high-rise apartment (more like an interior mansion) in the most elite residential neighborhood in Cleveland and a marriage to his pretty, blonde college sweetheart.

What is the plan?

There is none as Jewel wanders into the living room, appearing as if in a dream state. But not. Awake is a dream state illuminated. However, Jewel does not know this yet. She does not even know why she places a letter in an envelope on the dining room table in front of Dan's prized mirror.

Such a simple act.

The fear is present, rising like bile. But her resolve remains. *I am running for my life.* Yet Jewel's pace is slow and steady. No one could ever guess that the world just broke open.

The envelope simply said, "Dan," not "Daniel" and certainly not "My Dan" or even the formal "Daniel Goldberg." No, "Dan" was right. Unassuming. To the point. The note inside was also simple and to the point. It wrote itself.

"Slums are bad for poor people ..."

This was a line she had heard while they were watching the seven o'clock news. She remembered thinking, *How poignant*, as Dan laughed and, with a flick of his hand, pronounced, "That's ridiculous."

So, she began with that line. Because, really, that moment was the sum of it all. And then she wrote ...

> Cages are bad for animals,
> and marriage is bad for women.
> Truly,
> Jewel

Jewel stands by the hall door to their apartment and listens. She waits. A few minutes. An hour. A lifetime. She waits for something to happen. A memory trigger. But the only sound is that of her breath, her heartbeat, and the hallway breeze playing with the hairs on her forearms.

She has never been a courageous woman, always overidentifying with the Cowardly Lion in the *Wizard of Oz*. "I may not come out alive, but I'm going in there. There's only one thing I want you fellows to do ... Talk me out of it!"

Is it too late or not late enough?

She locks the door to their apartment. The click sound reverberates down the hall. The elevator going down drops her into the large parking garage. *Beep* ... The Ford Focus door opens. She throws her one bag in the back seat and checks the full envelope in her pocketbook. Five thousand dollars. That's it. That's all she took. The key slides into the ignition, the floor grip shifts to reverse, then transfers to drive, and before she knows it, the car is off ... to see the wizard?

Chapter 16

Drive, Damn It!

In the car, she tries to make sense of all of it. But what does making sense really mean? The whole presumption is that there is an order that everyone agrees upon. And if you're not a part of that world, the world of sense, you don't make any—sense, that is.

More than several times, she turns her Focus around, leaves the highway, and returns in the direction of Cleveland. She should have said something to Dan. But what? What could she say? Words appear as if written across her brain. A whole sentence from the book left on the pavement in front of Café Noir, underlined in pink. By Nancy? "The whole of life is about another chance, and while we are alive, till the very end, there is always another chance."

If only she could have said that to Dan. Would he understand? He didn't need to be angry at women. He didn't need to hide his love. Jewel was giving him that chance. She is giving herself that chance. In that moment, she forgave him. But could she forgive herself?

For God's sake, Jewel, do the right thing!

Jewel pulls the Focus over. She stops, lays her head on the wheel, and sobs. *Do the right thing.* She pulls her head off the wheel after a good ten-minute cry. She can't remember when she has cried like this in her adult life. When did bawling your eyes out become obsolete?

Then she engages in a serious conversation with herself. The old self and the new.

Old Self: "For God's sake, Jewel, what's gotten into you? Do the right thing."

New: "There is a difference between doing the right thing and doing the right thing."

Old Self: "What the hell. That is something New would say. The right thing is going back to Dan, your husband of thirty years. The right thing is pretending this never happened. The right thing is being a good wife. The right thing is being a pillar in your community. And you are, my dear. You were and can be again."

New: "Yes, that's the first right thing—a life of pretension. Old Self is good at that. Not being able to talk about what's really on your mind, even the books you read. Being the good wife, you didn't even notice that your own husband wasn't sleeping with you. You can only live a lie so long."

Old Self: "Oh please. Do you forget that you had such a hard life before Dan? The loss of both parents, foster homes, and poverty. Who the hell wants to live like that? Dan was the best decision you ever made. Choose me over madness. Because that is your choice, and New knows it. Don't ya, New?

New: "You're right, Old Self. I can't guarantee sanity. I can't guarantee anything."

Old Self: "See? I told you. I am safe. I am protected. I am what you know. Who would purposely walk off a cliff?"

New: "Crazy, huh? Walking off a cliff."

Old Self: "Well, I'm glad you finally admit it. It's fuckin' crazy."

New: "Do you want to know what the other right thing is?"

Old Self: "Oh, please do enlighten us."

New: "It's the opposite of what everyone tells you. It's something you know inside. A smile. A real conversation. A good book."

Old Self: "You forgot dead people visiting. A café that disappears. The loss of a husband who has provided well for you. Look in the mirror, Jewel."

Jewel glances at herself in the car mirror.

Old Self: "What happened to that pretty blonde? An outstanding member of the community. What happened to your figure? Look at all that gray. It's appalling."

Jewel nods. *You are so right. What the fuck am I doing? I've gone completely insane. That's what.*

Old Self, gleefully: "Sometimes it's so difficult always being right. Who am I kidding? That's what my life is about. It's time we go home where we belong. Drive, damn it!"

Movement calms Jewel. The motion of going forward or backward or somewhere. The Ford Focus moves of its own accord.

She barely notices the sign for Pennsylvania or Connecticut. Before she realizes it (although it has been hours), Jewel reaches her destination.

Okay, this is interesting ... Now it's time to turn back. Just turn the damn Ford Focus around.

Instead, Jewel lifts her arms in the air and in one deep breath whispers ...

"I am here!"

I

Going mad takes time.
Getting sane takes time.
—Jeanette Winterson

Chapter 1

When in Doubt

I pull my Focus into a crowded, free parking lot with a two-hour limit. And I sit. I am frozen in the Focus, absolutely numb from the waist down. As I open the glove compartment to retrieve my wallet, now with five thousand dollars cash, my book with the unfinished title flies out. When I pick it up, a thickly rolled joint falls from the pages. A gift from Jerry Schwartz, I suppose. I kiss it into the air and pay my regards to the man who left it. *Thank you, Jerry.*

I frantically search the car for a book of matches, find one with two lonely matches inside, light the joint, and take a toke. The book title stares at me from the passenger seat, *There But For The*. Perfect. I am truly the unfinished woman. No credit cards, no cell, no husband, no home, no friends, and no bank account. What the hell? I take another (this time considerably longer) toke. I don't need much at this age to get high. Now I really can't move. "What the hell," I say out loud in a remarkably different tone and with attitude.

I move to the passenger seat so I can plop my feet on the dashboard. There. And smoke some more. I remember from my college days the feeling of being stoned. I look up at the sky. There are no clouds. A baby-blue blanket covers me. The beauty of it all. A tear falls down my cheek. I give it a quick wipe. This is me, the old, the new, the in between. It's all me. Just one moon. Though fully clothed, I am naked and scared shitless and beautiful. Where is Dan now? I push him away because I really loved him once. Once in a dream.

Right now, I can't feel my toes. That's more than a little frightening. Toes … an odd word. I'd like to call them my Joes. Getting my Joes pedicured. The highlight of my week.

Vacuous. I'm fuckin' vacuous.

You might ask yourself … I'm talking to the sky now. How does one get this way? Well, I know exactly how. It starts small. At first, I pretended in order not to feel so out of place. In the community. In the life. In the marriage. I defended it, at least to myself. I excelled at it. I became it.

It's as simple as that. The game is no longer a game. The lie is no longer a lie. I embodied pretension. It was my anchor and my armor. And I reaped the benefits.

I open the car door on the passenger side and attempt to get out of the Focus. A deafening applause erupts from the parking lot. All the drivers are standing by their respective cars. Are they congratulating me? A woman with tangled locks and mismatched clothes yells, "You go, girl!" An old man, bent over with a cane in his hand, raises it and with a hoarse voice screams, "Amazing!" A young girl with old-fashioned Doc Martins and purple hair shouts, "You're not in Kansas anymore!" I bow and fall back into the passenger seat.

Who am I kidding? Wake up, damn it! No one, absolutely no one, gives you kudos for making a big change in your life that has nothing to do with greed or power. The real hard stuff never gets applauded—even by friends, especially those closest to you. People don't like their boat rocked. The old self knows this all too well.

I look up. The sky is still blue and cloudless. The sun warms my cheeks and forehead. My mouth is dry. I swallow. I take a whiff under my arms. Not so bad. I inhale a long, deep belly breath, slowly exhale, and stand. I stand for a few seconds. I am upright and grounded by the pavement. I reach for my dark glasses in my Luis Vuitton purse and hide behind their protection. I am nobody. I am invisible.

I take my first step. My body is wobbly. I'm not sure if it's the pot or a baby step of my new self. My hands smooth down my wrinkled clothes, and the shoulder strap of my bag travels across my left shoulder of its own accord. Old helps New get a grip. "You need something familiar," Old whispers. New nods in agreement.

The next thing I know, I am walking into a used clothing shop, Boomerangs. "When in doubt, go shopping," Old Self gently reminds us. The three of us smile in unison.

Chapter 2

Wings, Color, and
Barry Manilow

The lights in the used clothing store brighten as I walk in. I mean, suddenly they are blazing. I'm not making this up. This is not my imagination playing tricks like the episode in the parking lot. I walk in—and boom. I look over to the clerk to see if she notices. Did she just wink at me? I watch her as she manipulates the lights behind and to the right of the counter. I look at her with my fingers above my eyes. Too bright, I gesture. She smiles and tones them down.

The theatre of my new life begins. I have my own lighting person. And an audience, even though I know they are only pretend. "This is my movie, my play," I vow to the store merchandise. A surge of energy whips through my body. I am out of control and in control at the same time, a real, living paradox. I grab a few articles of clothing in my size, even a name brand here and there, and place a straw fedora on my head. I throw my scarf, Amita's scarf, over my shoulder.

"Whoa," I hear. When I turn around, I realize that another customer is shadowing me, practically on top of me. The scarf must have brushed her face.

"I love your fedora and your scarf like the sea!" she shrieks. "The whole ensemble!"

I step back a few inches before I thank her.

"Close your eyes." She is mouthing the words.

"What?"

"Close your eyes. Do you like surprises?"

"I don't know …"

"You won't believe what I just found. But I won't show it to you unless you …"

"Close my eyes."

I close my eyes. Right there in the middle of Boomerangs. I had picked up a few affordable purchases for my journey to nowhere and thought, *Why the hell not?*

"Wait a minute," she announces. "Open them again. I just want you to understand that my outfit doesn't really fit with what I bought."

Truth be told, her outfit wouldn't fit with anything. She is wearing red flowered pajama pants, a brown checked shirt, and pink rubber boots. In fact, she looks uncannily familiar. She resembles the woman with mismatched clothes in the parking lot. How can that be?

She interrupts my reverie, apologizing. "You'll have to excuse it."

I smile. I mean, I know she is as crazy as they come, but her energy is catching. Her strange familiarity is comforting somehow. Also, she seems bright and alive and full of surprises. More than that, I feel my first real smile in days, weeks—damn, maybe even months.

I close my eyes for what seems to be at least ten minutes. What the hell is she doing? They open.

"Uh, uh, uh," she admonishes.

They shut. Something in me is just too used to taking orders. But this is, I don't know, more like a game. Hide-and-seek without hiding or seeking.

"Okay, you can open them now. I'm ready."

My eyes openly obey.

"Voila!" she exclaims.

I am speechless for a second. And then I utter in a hushed tone, "Wings."

She corroborates as she gleefully flaps her plastic butterfly wings. "Yes, yes, and do you believe I discovered them right here in Boomerangs—a used clothing store, for heaven's sake?"

I can't help but stare. I'm certain my mouth is agape. There is something so beautifully bizarre about this woman.

She laughs. "You are my witness." The lady, half butterfly / half woman, circles me, flaps her wings, and flies out of Boomerangs.

***

"Close your eyes."

Not again. What is this? I am sitting in one of those massage chairs that is poking and knuckling all the wrong places, creating aches I was not aware I even had, smack-dab in the middle of Nails Are Us, conveniently located next door to Boomerangs on Centre Street in Jamaica Plain. At this moment, I'm having a minor (maybe not so minor) nervous breakdown. Willow Green? Purple Grapes? Yellow as Corn? Orange Shock? I want something new, but what? Anything but Blushing Pink or Real Red? "Not what was," I say to myself. "But what is?"

"This has never been a problem before," I restate to the manicurist in front of me. "I always know what I want."

She looks at me with a mischievous smile. "Things have changed. I know change," she says in accented but clear English. "I only arrived here from Vietnam three years ago. I'm staying with my cousin."

Then she tells me her name in Vietnamese, but she wants me to call her by her American translation.

"Call me Banana. That is my American name."

"I love it."

"It's not quite the exact translation, but it always makes for a smile."

She has no idea, or maybe she does, how important a smile is to me.

"Now, close your eyes and keep them closed."

My eyes slowly close.

"You are totally in my hands now. I am in control."

I am hoping that I appear to be letting go, but I feel my body tensing up. I really have no clue how to let go. Banana senses my tension and adjusts the speed of the massage chair, which is now bullying every muscle in my body.

Curiosity, or is it fear, gets the best of me, and my eyes pop open.

"No, no. You are totally in my hands now. Keep your eyes closed," she demands.

This should be a piece of cake for me. After all, I trusted my husband for thirty years of my life without question. But then again, it was also without forethought. Anyway, this is not a marriage. I'm giving my nails over for an hour for Christ's sake. It's sort of like trusting the universe, as my old friends from college would say. My husband would be totally opposed to this scenario. I close my eyes gladly for once.

Banana finally shuts the chair completely off. She knows. The knowing makes me like her even more. She is kind of quirky and smart and brave. It is suddenly so easy. My heart relaxes, my muscles, even my bones, and before I know it …

"Okay. Open your eyes."

I hear her faintly.

"You can open your eyes now."

They leisurely open.

"You were asleep."

"Yes, I was." Then I look down at my toes. "Wow!" I exclaim. My left big toe is green, the toe next to it is purple, then green, and so on. My right big toe is purple, then green, and so on. There is a method to her madness.

"You like?" she asks.

"It is brilliant. Do the exact same thing for my manicure."

"Do you like?" she asks the entire salon as she parades me, her explosion of creativity, around the room. I am being showcased by Banana. I feel like a star. Her star.

When she sits me down to do my manicure, she kisses me unabashedly on the cheek and whispers in my ear, "Thank you."

And I wonder, if not just for a second, where the life of thank you begins and where it ends.

***

This time, it is all too obvious. After all, you must close your eyes when getting your hair washed. But it is the way he speaks. His Brazilian accent is soft and sweet. It reminds me of sands and ocean and the breeze on a summer's day. So, when he sings, *"Close your eyes,"* I do so gladly.

"Do you like stories?" he asks.

An odd question. However, now that books of fiction have provoked such a huge shift in my life, leaving a thirty-year marriage, I have gained a new and deeply profound respect for the story.

"I love stories," I eagerly volunteer.

"Do you write?"

"Well, I used to write poetry when I was young."

"I knew it. I just knew it!" he announces, a little loudly. I can feel the sudden silence in the room.

"Why not now?"

"What?"

"Why do you not write poetry now?"

"Maybe I do." My own words surprise me.

"I am writing a story …" He pauses.

He has my full attention.

"My wife is going to translate into English …"

His wife? I thought for sure he was gay. But then again, I was certain that my husband wasn't.

"It is about a healer in Brazil, Maria. My mother took me to her in my teens because I had no direction. She was eighty-nine years old but had the agility of a forty-year-old. She walked me through her woods and picked herbs. She told me about each herb as she chose carefully. When we returned to her small cabin, she put them in a pot and made tea. Many things happened in the next hours, which will be in my story. But one of the most memorable parts was how she touched me. She dipped her fingers in the mashed herbs and rubbed her hands together as if washing them. She massaged my cheeks, forehead, ears, bridge of my nose, eyes, somehow knowing all the places that desperately needed to be soothed and, yes, freed."

The scent of the shampoo is stronger as he speaks, as if I'm inhaling mint and lavender straight into my nostrils. I panic slightly.

"You must relax." It is not, in any way, a demand. His words, like velvet, calm me immediately.

The story continues. "Maria told me stories of healers. I asked her how she became a healer. She told me, 'I come from a family of healers. It passes through me like it passes through you.'"

"Maria told you that you were a healer?"

"I wasn't sure, so I asked her if she was saying that I also have powers. In Brazil, there are many that find they have power later in life. I was still only a teenager. But Maria just smiled, a rather large, toothless smile."

"And then what happened?"

"We talked about trees and plants. It was like the school lessons but much grander. She told me stories into the evening and into the next morning under the copaiba tree, and then we both closed our eyes. I had never slept so soundly."

He places his warm, fragrant hands over my eyes and then massages my scalp, harder than I am used to. I know this will sound strange, but let's face it: the whole day has been like this. I feel as if he is literally pulling fodder out of my brain. I feel empty, in a good way, for the first time in my life.

My eyes remain closed, as I too am taken under the copaiba tree. Maria passes me a cup of tea. It is a little bitter and burns my throat but tastes sweeter as I drink. We are silent for what seems like hours but can only really be a few seconds. Both of our eyes are closed, and we are breathing in unison. She begins to hum. The song feels familiar somehow, but I don't recognize it. Her humming is slow at first. I am lulled into a sweet afternoon nap. And just when I am about to fall deeply, her pace quickens. She shakes her head, moves her arms and hands, and bursts into song …

Her name is Lola
She was a showgirl
With yellow feathers in her hair
And a dress cut down to there
She would meringue
And do the cha-cha
And while she tried to be a star
Tony always tended bar
Across the crowded room
They worked from eight to four ...

My eyes burst open. "What?"

The young man is towel drying my hair. "I am finished. You must have fallen asleep."

He walks me to the hairdresser's chair. All I can say is, "I had the strangest dream."

"Do you think so?"

"The whole day ..."

"My name is Paulo Roberto, but you can call me by my nickname, Beto."

"Beto ..."

"In Brazil, we don't make all those distinctions ... between dream and awake."

Beto adjusts the towel on my shoulders and states matter-of-factly, "And personally, if I never hear another Barry Manilow tune again, it won't be soon enough for me."

Michelle A. Gabow

Chapter 3

Stepfriends

"She hurriedly ran up the steps. Well, let me backtrack a second. There were these steps at the Arborway Arboretum. Flowers, purple chrysanthemums, velvet red roses, and bright yellow daffodils dressed the stone stairway all the way up. Bursts of color and beauty. She couldn't see the top of the staircase, so she ran up. She just imagined the magnificent bouquet and splendor she would envision on top. But each time she thought she made it to the top, there were more steps. 'A staircase to nowhere,' she whispered. She kept running. Like a *Road Runner* cartoon, more would appear. This was absolutely crazy. She desperately wanted to get to the top until she realized, exhausted and totally out of breath, there was no top. So, she decided to descend. But when she looked down to where she had come from, all the steps behind her were gone. They had disappeared. She panicked. What the hell was happening? She was dangling on the last cement step in midair, crying for help. There wasn't a soul around. 'My God,' she screamed. 'Where are the people? Such a glorious park, and there is no one here to enjoy it!' Slowly her step, the one that was holding her, began to disintegrate, chipping off the sides, turning into sand. What had she done? Why couldn't she stay at the bottom where she belonged?

She had trouble breathing. She was going to fall. She was going to die. And she was all alone."

"See," interjects Banana. "That's the point. You are not alone."

Maybe I should backtrack again. I do need to set somewhat of a scene. I mean, that's not how truth comes, in order, in scenes. Though I could never tell Dan that. But I'm still a little old-fashioned in my storytelling or truth telling. I have a strong desire to answer some questions first.

How did I end up in Jamaica Plain, Massachusetts?

Good question. I kind of skipped that part of the narrative. I think it's good to know how you came to land where you landed. I never examined that question when I was with Dan. What is that quote about an unexamined life? No matter. It's the fear of examining that is my point, the fear of what lurked inside the perfect package. This fear strangled but never left our upper-class throats—fear not only of our lies but also of an intangible terror of the unknown.

I have a vivid memory of a conversation that took place eight years ago. Amazing what stays in our heads. It is of Myrna telling me confidentially, in almost a whisper, that her brilliant, Harvard-educated daughter dropped out of school to become a performance artist. She had moved out of Cambridge to a neighborhood called Jamaica Plain, a neighborhood Myrna would not set foot in. It sounded strangely exciting, artsy, warm, and diverse, and maybe even affordable. I was riding in my car to nowhere when I thought, *This is the direction from one dropout to another.* Maybe I would drop into Jamaica Plain. The neighborhood appeared to have all the above except the most important criterion. It was not cheap. Things had changed in eight years. Gentrification moves at a frightening, life-altering speed. I should know. However, from my first day's events, I knew magic was in the air.

Question number two: am I afraid that my husband will find me?

The answer is simply no. I created the ideal closet for Dan, the victim, the perfect husband. He can live his lifestyle choice in less fear. He is thanking me at this moment, probably having a good laugh on my account. You're so welcome, Danny boy.

Question number three: what makes me think I can live on five thousand dollars?

I didn't ... think ... that is.

And the last question, question number four: how am I living?

Ahh ... A miracle flew into my life! Yes, a real miracle with wings. I bumped into her at the market, the same woman who entertained me at Boomerangs, the used clothing store, the day before. She had probably left her wings in the car. I was so thrilled to see her, my first real contact in Jamaica Plain. I excitedly ran up to her. "You're the lady with wings!"

She looked at me, rather bewildered. It was clear that she didn't recognize me. I could understand that. I mean, I'm a middle-aged woman, dressed like a middle-aged woman. My pizzazz level, even my phony, thin pizzazz level, was gone. I was at an in-between stage. I like to think of it as the stage before a caterpillar changes into a butterfly.

Then she looked at me again, out of the corner of her eye. "I left my wings in the car."

I knew that.

"Do you live around here?" she nonchalantly asked.

"I don't live anywhere at the moment."

Her face flushed with enthusiasm. "You're running away!"

How did she know?

"Oh, you poor dear. We need to hide you."

"I really don't need to hi—"

"And I just happen to have the perfect place. Follow me."

Now in my regular life, my old life, I would have never in a million years followed someone who was apparently quite bonkers. However, this was my new life. I followed her and quickly. She walked at a pace that was difficult to keep up with, but I managed to be only a few steps behind. As she opened the doors to her 1960 Chevy Impala, I noticed her wings were, in fact, resting on the back seat. I was eternally grateful because my Focus had recently died on Centre Street, minus the registration and license plate, which I carefully removed. She drove me to an old house that sat back on a small, winding street called Williams. The house was large, like an old mansion, and slightly unkempt looking on the outside but beautiful no less.

"What do you think?" she asked while walking me through the oak door.

"I think that I really can't afford to stay here."

She waved her hand and admonished, "That's ridiculous."

We walked into a magnificent old house full of the original wood, sparsely furnished with what looked like found objects and an early seventies flair. Print scarves over lamps, Indian bedspreads covering tables and chairs, beads hanging in doorways between rooms, and surprisingly clean.

"Let me take you to your room."

"My room?"

She led me into an attic bedroom that was almost round, surrounded with windows, no curtains. It had one wrought iron single bed and a mahogany wood bureau. It was marvelously empty. And again, amazingly clean.

All I could say was, "Wow, this is spotless."

"I'm pretty OCD, as well as a few other things." She laughed a hearty laugh.

"How much are you charging for rent?"

"How much do you have?"

"I left home with about five thousand dollars in cash. I have pretty close to that now."

"The truth is I don't need the cash. I'm leaving for parts unknown in a few months, and I need someone responsible to mind the house. You're perfect for the role."

"Where are you going?"

"I never tell anyone where I'm going. You are not an exception."

"You're asking me to live here without rent?"

"Yes."

"I don't even know your name."

"What month is this?"

"July."

"Last month, my name was June. I change every month. You can call me Sparrow for this month."

June Last Month, Sparrow This Month was not what she appeared to be, or maybe she was. She had a beautiful home that she rarely lived in and probably came from some family money. I realized Sparrow had a craziness only old wealth could afford. I was not frightened of her. There was something sweet and kind about her. Even the intense lines on her face reflected a profound gentleness. The hard facts were I had no place to stay, I had little money, and if this got weird, which was a real possibility, I could leave. I was not marrying Sparrow. I was not marrying anybody, thank God. So Sparrow This Month and I shook hands on the deal. "By the way, my name is Jewel."

Her only response was, "Of course."

After my first few days in our home, Sparrow told me that we must have a housewarming and suggested I invite a few friends. She claimed not to have any.

Okay, that brings me here, now, having wine with my three new friends. I was only a little surprised when Banana and Beto both accepted my invitation so graciously. After all, I had only just met them. Yet there was something almost primal about these beginning friendships. I felt it, and I knew they felt it too. This was part of the new me, this unconditional knowing at the oddest moments. I recognized kindred spirits; we were all on the precipice of something in our mutual lives. Our connection made no sense in the real world. Yet they accepted my invitation without hesitation. And here all four of us were, dissecting a dream.

ME: What I want to know is what was her hurry, and why was she running up the steps?

SPARROW THIS MONTH: I don't think that should be the question.

BETO: Me neither.

SPARROW THIS MONTH: Why she?

ME: What?

BETO: Why do you talk about yourself in third person? She is you.

ME: It seems that I've been living in third person for a greater portion of my life than I care to admit.

Sparrow This Month refills all our wine glasses. I don't know about the others, but I am well on my way to being totally plastered.

ME: I've been in goddamn third person all my goddamn life.

Beto ruptures into laughter. His laugh sounds as if he is sneezing and hiccupping simultaneously. The whole group disintegrates into a bizarre, lengthy laugh. There is a long pause in the conversation as we slowly return to our breathing. Banana is the first to speak.

BANANA: That's why you were running. We are all running up the steps. There's something more to this life, this journey, don't you think? And it's uphill. Maybe the only thing holding us up is our courage to look. Maybe it's each other. Maybe that's why we all met.

She pauses.

BANANA: I just don't want to do nails forever.

ME: You are an artist!

Banana just smiles. A tear falls from the corner of her right eye.

BANANA: You are my first American friends.

BETO: Mine too. In some ways, Maria, a healer from my community, sent me here. It was like, after seeing her, I just knew. Not everything, just that the United States was my direction. And that she is part of my story. A story I have to write. A story I only shared with my wife and Jewel and now all of you. But I am frightened of this new life.

BANANA: Terror. I'm been, how do I say …

SPARROW THIS MONTH: In a state of terror …

BANANA: Yes, I've been in a state of terror for three years, since I arrived in the States.

Sparrow This Month refills our glasses.

SPARROW THIS MONTH: I know terror. Sometimes we need to go that place. Terror signals us that we, in fact, exist. We have to use the terror in our dreams, both awake and in sleep. It is a strange and powerful form of trust. It is in the face of terror that we create. To run away or not to look is not living. I now welcome terror because in order to be reborn, we have to let go, we have to face our fear, we have to die.

We all fall silent.

ME: The steps turning into sand below my feet!

SPARROW THIS MONTH: Yes!

There is a whisper from Banana, but I cannot detect the words; it is so soft.

SPARROW THIS MONTH: What? Speak up.

BANANA: I have a secret.

SPARROW THIS MONTH: Oh how delicious.

BANANA: Not even my aunt or my cousins know, who I live with now.

Our backs straighten with anticipation.

BANANA: I have rented a cheap studio so I can paint. It is in the old Sam Adams factory. It doesn't have heat, but …

SPARROW THIS MONTH: It's a room of your own.

ME: Virginia Woolf.

I think I'm becoming a little obnoxious with this whole reading thing.

BANANA: When I am in the studio, everything else disappears.

ME: That's how I feel when I read something powerful. Everything around me disappears. There is timelessness. Or a new sense of time.

For me, this has been the most powerful discovery. So, to say it out loud makes me want to explode.

BETO: When I'm writing about Maria, it's like I'm not alone in the room, but I am alone. A kind of bubble surrounds me. I can't hear anything or see anything, but I'm opening to this story, my story again. My wife says she can say the most outrageous things, and I don't hear her. The more I think of it, it really isn't a bubble. It's almost as if I'm more in the world, in the universe, than I've ever been.

SPARROW THIS MONTH: Yes, yes. That's so fuckin' true. That's how I feel when I'm flying.

All three of us look at her quizzically.

Sparrow This Month, June Last gives us a big, toothless smile and empties the bottle of wine into our glasses.

SPARROW THIS MONTH: Let's toast to our new selves.

We click our glasses.

SPARROW THIS MONTH: And new adventures. I will be leaving tomorrow.

ME, BETO, BANANA: Tomorrow?

BANANA: But … we are just becoming friends.

SPARROW THIS MONTH: We are friends. Every time you three come together, this, tonight, will be a part of our friendship … And of course, I always come back.

BETO: I hate change.

SPARROW THIS MONTH: Oh shit. Look at us. Change is who we are, my darlings.

ME: I won't even know your new name.

SPARROW THIS MONTH: Well, pick a name, any name.

BANANA: I think it is Wisdom.

BETO: Or Truth!

I grab Sparrow's hand to hold her here with us just a little longer. June Last Month, Sparrow This immediately shines. Her cheeks emanate a rose glow, her eyes glisten, and her few crooked teeth break out of their shell, as if one could see into her soul. I have never witnessed such unrestrained beauty, such light. What passes quickly through my mind is one simple fact about Sparrow. This moment with the three of us is possibly the first time she has ever been seen—I mean really seen. Some people choose to hide themselves; others flaunt themselves and in essence do the same thing. But June Last Month is invisible because the world refuses to look. She is so much who she is that it borders on an enchanting, rich, and unabashed insanity. We spend our whole life in fear of our own madness. I am now sitting next to and living in a home with my greatest fear. What a goddamn gift. We all must have perceived this at the same time because Beto speaks directly to it.

BETO: To Sol, the Portuguese word for the sun and its light.

ALL: To Sol Next Month.

That is our last toast of the night. After a long goodbye, I barely saunter up the staircase, literally tripping into my room.

I am about to fall into a thoughtful slumber in my single wrought iron bed. Feeling wonderfully inebriated, I notice a large shadow pass through all the surrounding windows. My eyes close, and I drift off to the sound of wings flapping into the night. The following morning, Sparrow This Month, Sol Next is gone.

Chapter 4

Cheap Cologne and Stale Cigarettes

"The hallway stinks of cheap cologne and stale cigarettes. What the hell is going on here? Wake up! Why are you napping in the afternoon in my living room? Who the hell are you?"

"I am your wife."

"You don't look anything like my wife."

"That's true, but nevertheless …"

"Nevertheless … there's bird crap all over the house. Is there some sort of, I don't know … giant bird living here … Did you hear that?"

"What?"

"Wings flapping."

"I didn't hear a thing."

"Bullshit!"

My eyes fling open. Where did Dan go? I call his name, "Dan, Dan, where are you? I'm so sorry. Do you hear me? I said I'm …" I'm all alone. I can hardly breathe. I'm all alone in this big house. I grab the pack of Camels lying on the coffee table. I slip out a cigarette and light it with the lighter next to it. I sit up on the sofa. It feels soft to the touch. I love that Sparrow has a purple velvet sofa. It is something I would have chosen for this room if I wasn't with my husband, Dan, because he would hate it. "It looks like a sofa you'd find in a brothel!" But I'm not with Dan; I love this sofa. And I'm smoking a Camel cigarette even if it kills me. Better than slowly strangling in someone else's life.

I glance around this living room. It's large and in some ways kind of fantastic. The colors are soft grays, purples, and pale greens with hints of Chinese red and burnt orange. The furniture is totally disconnected, and in fact that's what connects them. A Victorian sofa, an art nouveau coffee table, an old, worn wicker chair, a La-Z-Boy recliner, a single futon on the floor, covered with a red and orange Indian print bedspread and a wild assortment of pillows. Brightly colored sixties glass beads hang from all the doorways. The windows are provocatively naked. Scarves decorate the tables, chairs, and walls. I am sitting in the middle of a life I know nothing about. Everything in it, including me, feels found. I don't know what to do with myself. I know what I'm not doing. I'm not making Dan his morning coffee and lightly toasted bagel. I'm not cleaning the house to Dan's perfection. I'm not gossiping with the women I thought of as friends. I'm not organizing fund drives or working out at the gym. Nothing is known to me. And I am the biggest unknown of all.

What the hell am I doing?

I crush my lit cigarette into the glass ashtray. My mind is blank. The house, even inside my brain, is now silent. I am sitting hunched over, chin resting in my open hands, arms resting on the coffee table. Nothing is happening for a long time. Light still streams into the room, so it is clearly not evening yet. Nothing. Then I notice a hummingbird in the window. Dancing still. I stare at the beauty of her dance. I swear she is looking back. We are each other's mirrors for a few moments, and then she is gone, as if she was just lifted right out of the window's frame. I am about to light another Camel when I smell cigarette—or is it cigar smoke? I check my Camel in the ashtray. It is definitely out, but I mash it some more. It is in pieces. I walk the ashtray over to the kitchen garbage can and empty it. The stench is stronger. In fact, the house reeks of a cigarette in progress. I follow the smoke. I'm terrified. I may not be alone.

I walk up the stairs slowly, following the aroma of tobacco like strange breadcrumbs. As I tiptoe, each step cracks. There's no such thing as total silence in an old house; every floorboard has an old bruise and a story to tell. That is what I loved and now hate about my new home. I realize I should be carrying a large baseball bat or a can of Mace, but I haven't a clue to where any of these necessities would be kept. Note to myself: buy a can of Mace and baseball bat tomorrow. There is a buzzing sound close to my ear. I am distracted, almost dizzy. I trip on one of the steps. I stand, and something flies in front of my face, too close. I can't quite take it in. It lifts up. I look up. It's the hummingbird. How the hell did it get in? The smoke is wafting closer, much closer. I want to call Banana and tell her that I completely get terror. The smoke is definitely coming from Sparrow's bedroom. Immediately, my whole body relaxes. Damn it, she's been here the whole time. I can breathe again. I collect myself. I don't want her to think she has a *crazy* living with her. I picture June Last Month, the day I met her modeling her wings, and burst out laughing. I just want to give her a hug. I peer into Sparrow This Month's room and freeze. I am unable to move in any direction from the doorway. I am an immovable rock of pure panic. Sparrow is not the one sitting on the bed, smoking a cigarette, and drinking what appears to be rum.

"Do not walk through a doorway with that energy," admonishes the woman on the bed, already a few sheets to the wind. "In Brazil, we know how to treat a traveler and a guest." Maria smiles a beautiful, toothless grin. "And it's not like we haven't met."

"Does Beto know you are here?"

"Well, I would hope so."

"A little early to be drinking," I say from the doorway.

"Yes, it is."

I stand in the doorway a few moments. Maria does not invite me in but pours another glass from a bottle of rum.

"Where did you get that?" I question from my spot in the doorway.

"From under your kitchen sink."

"It's not *my* kitchen sink. This is not even *my* house."

Maria laughs. "Are you scared that if you step through that doorway, you'll never come back?"

"No ... well, maybe. Yes, I'm terrified. My life seems to be going in that direction."

Maria pats a spot on the bed in front of her with her unoccupied hand. I walk in and sit across from her on the bed. She passes me the recently filled glass of rum and grabs her own from the floor. She folds her legs and smiles. I fold mine. I don't know what to do next. We sit in relative silence. I decide to make conversation.

"I've been reading a lot lately."

"Is that so," Maria replies while putting down her drink and lighting a cigar. She picks up her rum, again from the floor; the glass of rum is now in her left hand, and the cigar in her right.

"I mean, I've always read. But now it's different. Completely different."

Maria takes a long drag of her cigar. The smoke comes out in circles. It is very impressive. I have never been able to exhale with such finesse. I watch the circles for a few seconds. They turn colors in the air, almost like small released rainbows from Maria's mouth. I'm beginning to wonder if she didn't put a little something in my drink.

"Herbs," she answers before I ask. "All natural."

I let it pass. I don't know why. Maybe because I have a story to tell and am anxious to tell it. "You see, now, reading has taken on a whole new life. The books have become like ... premonitions. They are foreshadowing my life. Some kind of a very kinky map. I know it sounds *kinda* bizarre ..."

Maria swigs down a full glass of rum in one fluid motion. While renewing her glass, she pours more in mine, which already has plenty. However, it is clear I have her full attention. In fact, I can't remember when I have captured someone's attention quite like this. More like never in my life. I feel this electricity between us and in my body. My entire self from toe to head can no longer keep my story inside. It's a heavy rock and light as a feather. Maria is eager and willing to catch either.

"I'm reading Patty Smith, *M Train*. Here I am in this house, and this book literally falls from the shelf. Just falls in front of me. It actually lifts itself off the shelf and blocks my way. I have to pick it up. And it's not the first time this has happened."

I pause for effect. There is none, so I continue. "There is a line is this book that says, 'The dead speak. We have forgotten how to listen.' Do you believe that a dead person can speak?"

"Don't be ridiculous. I'm Brazilian. The dead can be very talkative and funny and wise and, at times, very angry. Sometimes I just have to shut them up."

"How do you do that?"

"I sing. That shuts everyone up." Maria breaks into laughter, more like cackling for a few seconds. And then silence.

I'm waiting for her to tell me to go on. But nothing. I realize I could wait all day. She doesn't have much in the manners department. So, I go on. I figure she'll sing me to silence if and when she wants to.

"Let me start at a beginning."

Maria takes a long drag of her cigar and a swig of her drink.

"About eight months ago, maybe more, I walked into a bookstore/café. Not really my style, but … well, it was my birthday, and something drew me in. The proprietor and a pretty fabulous barista, Nancy, and I became friends. But that day, on my table was a book. And I stole it when I left the café."

Maria puts down her drink and cigar on the shaky bed and claps.

"For that, you clap?"

"Of course, because you did not steal the book; the book stole you."

For a second, I couldn't continue. As simple as that sounded, I knew that she was right. It did steal me.

"And then I stole another. The book was *IQ84* by Haruku Murakmi. Murakmi writes about an alternative universe with two moons."

"Two moons," Maria replies, not as a question but just for slight emphasis.

"Yes. And I became obsessed." Pause. "So much so that I began living a double life."

"A second life."

"What's the difference?"

"One's a mystery."

"Thanks," is my sarcastic reply.

"A book doesn't solve the mystery."

"What does?"

"Living it."

"Is that what I'm doing? The truth is I don't know what the hell I'm doing. All I know is that because of that book, nothing was ever the same again."

Maria finally speaks. "A book is a book. You open it. You step through. Did you come back?"

"No, I didn't! Wait a minute. That's a line from a novel I've read."

"It's hard to be original when you're so intelligent."

"That's it. I was following the map."

"To home."

"No, to here."

Maria shrugs her shoulders and says (I think a little sarcastically also), "Right."

"I fought hard against following it until I was on the road, leaving my husband of thirty years. What I want to know from you … What I want to know from you, damn it, is am I a complete idiot?"

"Yes … good … an idiot … or else nothing happens. Life stands still."

"That was my little, perfectly right life."

"To always want to be right, to be right, is not living!" I am taken back by her emotional response. Maria wets her fingertips and puts out her cigar with her two fingers for emphasis. She continues to drink her rum. We sit quietly for a few minutes. She fills another glass for both of us. Again, mine still has rum and a little something I'm not sure of in it.

"My life is taking the shape of that book. I don't know what's real. Are you real or imagined?"

"Yes. A book is a doorway. A doorway is a doorway. You walk through. You wake up!"

I twist slightly to straighten the pillow holding my back, and when I turn around, Maria is gone. Poof. Vanished. Deserted the premises. The phone next to the bed is ringing. I pick it up.

A panicked Beto is on the other end. "Are you okay?"

"How did you kn—" Then I am silent. It's a question I am unable to answer with a yes or no. Finally, I declare, "Dan is right. I am not his wife."

There is a long pause. Then, as an afterthought, I add, "Maybe I never was.

Chapter 5

Maybe I Never Was

"I don't remember what happened on Thursday. I don't even remember Thursday. Then where did Friday go? I thought today was Friday."

Today is Sunday, or so Banana tells me while doing my nails. We call these our special visits, visits off the Nails Are Us premises. Visits where we can really talk. Banana, in her rented room, is a whole different species. I mean, she looks nothing like the girl I met in the nail salon. Though she loves her cousins, her first home in the States, she had to leave. She said that there was no way she could pursue herself in a place where they insisted they knew her.

We are a bunch of runaways.

Banana dips my fingers in lavender water. She sits across from me, an old wooden table between us. Her wig, which she calls "wigged-in," sits on the table. Banana in front of me looks nothing like her lovely wig, which is straight, long hair with bangs. Her hair is buzz cut on the sides; a heart shape is cut into one side in back of her right ear. Her blue-black hair is spiked with a flash of hot pink and much longer on the top. She has a few earrings in her right ear and none in her left. Her clothes are shades of black, and she wears white socks with bulky Doc Martin shoes. She is her art form.

"So, today is Sunday. You're sure."

"That's what the calendar says. I'm never sure."

"I really am losing track of time."

"You were tracking time?"

I know it's something about the idiom she doesn't get. However, she gets it perfectly.

Banana lightly wipes my right hand with a soft towel and tenderly drops my left hand into the water. She begins pushing back the cuticles, filing and shaping my nails. As I glance around her room, I notice a new unfinished painting hanging on her easel. The colors are gorgeous, pulsating, alive, yet with a touch of melancholy. Mostly the painting is filled with vibrant greens, but there is a sandy color throughout, pinks, a red here and there, and soft, pale gray-green shadows of figures, of family. She captured it all.

"Vietnam?" I ask.

"Yes."

Though abstract, it is clear. It is the waking dream. I want to ask how. How does she portray all that in a painting? But I am speechless. Or I think I am speechless because after some silence, she answers my unasked question. What is it about Maria, Beto, and now Banana that they can sense what's in the back of my brain and then respond to my thoughts? It's downright bizarre.

Banana reveals, "I take the name Banana—the name white people call me. And I stretch it into new shapes, new colors, new environments. But it's so easy to fold up. The terror is the lack of boundaries. I see so many of my friends from Vietnam, who came here to begin again, become what they were running away from. I don't fault them. Terror is a fucking monster."

Banana wipes my left hand with the towel. She massages my hands with a vanilla lotion. The combination of vanilla and lavender fills me. She lays out a few bottles of nail polish. "What color?"

And then I panic. "I don't know what goddamn color. I don't know what day it is! People visit and disappear. They become birds in the night. Strangers read my mind. Who am I? Who was I? I left a perfectly fine marriage. What the hell am I doing?"

"Close your eyes," whispers Banana.

"I ..."

"I'm here with you. Just gently shut them. Let them flutter and breathe."

I do.

"What do you hear?" she asks.

"A very loud electric lawn mower ... Silence. A few birds chirping. The wind, an airplane overhead, a distant dog bark, another bark, fire engines, a water faucet, a man on the phone, another dog bark, a car alarm, tools being put in a box, a creak on the floorboards, the engine of a car starting ... your cat breathing, curtains blowing in the wind ..."

"What do you smell?"

"Lavender, vanilla ... old wood, coffee, a powdered doughnut, just cut grass ..."

"What do you feel?"

"Your touch, sadness, silence, caressed, tired, not lonely ... a minor headache, a cramp in my foot, my heartbeat, a tear ..."

"Beyond any of those details of real, there are dreams. And everyone's living in them."

"Murakami."

"Of course."

Banana paints my nails. The polish is slightly cold and smells new. Everything is old. Everything is new. All at the same time. Banana responds to my thoughts.

"We are, only to become."

I sense she is finished. My eyes open. My fingernails are the palest of pale sky-blue, almost iridescent.

Banana smiles. "The sky has no limits."

Chapter 6

This Isn't That

"But there is one thing I could say for sure. No matter how you look at it, this isn't that world."

"It certainly isn't," I defiantly answer. I am sitting with this fifteen-hundred-page book in my lap, *IQ84*, my alternate reality, the two moons, begging me to open her up yet again. However, I can't. It's not that I'm frozen on this purple sofa or that the book is a weight that I can't lift. It's not that I'm purposely meditating or thinking about something else. However, I do find myself in this position more often than I care to admit. Sitting. Just sitting. Sometimes for hours. Once for an entire day.

In my other life, "that world," I basked on the fact that I was so active. *Idle hands are the devil's workshop.* Never did I just sit. I relished my *busyness.* It was my duty, my armor, my defining principle. It gave my life purpose. Dan used to joke, "My wife wouldn't know how to take a vacation," with this all-knowing grin, this strange pride.

The cheap bastard.

Who am I fooling? It was the closest thing to a compliment he ever gave me. And my back straightened, and my neck stretched as he uttered those words. Dan's overactive wife. Bouncy, energetic, a real dynamo.

So, when I finally opened the book toward its final pages, and these words leapt out, I knew it was true. "This isn't that world."

Something in me erupts, and I burst into song ... *Her name was Lola she was a showgirl with yellow flowers in her hair* ... I've never liked Barry Manilow, but somehow this tune has taken over my life. I move my body and start to dance all over the living room. I like the word, living room. A room that lives. And I want to live in it. Stretch. Take my body to new places. I do. This certainly isn't the gym, where body motions are separate from self and void of feeling. My gestures feel childlike. They seem to be rooted in emotion. My arms stretch, my heart beats, my legs kick all the shit, and especially Dan, out of the way, and my fingers and toes play music. Who is this woman dancing to her living? I throw off my clothes and twirl in circles. I am a Sufi, I am a fat goddess, I am ...

Loud disco music breaks my rhythm. My body is choked into another reality. I am blown back to the purple sofa. My breath catches until I realize that Beto programmed my cell phone, and this is the new ringtone. I search to find it, too late to answer but early enough to see the caller.

"Hi," I call and answer.

"Get dressed. Now," orders Banana.

How did she know that I was naked? How does Banana know all she knows? Does she really see through walls, my head, my thoughts?

"Now?" I question.

"We're going to lunch," she exclaims.

"To lunch ..."

"Yes, at Beto's place."

"Wow."

"Yes, I know. We'll finally meet Carly."

"I wonder what she's like. And why it took him so long to finally share her."

"We need to look ..." Banana was having trouble again with word retrieval.

"Fabulous," I said.

"Yes, fabulous. I'm walking over, and I am almost at your house. I'll pick you up in five minutes."

"You want a fifty-five-year-old woman to look fabulous in five minutes."

"Absolutely."

I don't shower. After all, I have five minutes. *Not showering ... never happened in that life.* I throw on an orange shift just below the knee, powder under my arms, lotion my body and face, gel my hair, and stop to admire Beto's new cut. He has graduated from hair washer to hairdresser and is amazing. Short, short gray hair on the sides, and platinum streaks scurry through the top that is much longer and wild. I run to Sol This Month's bedroom, empty of nothing except her, throw on an Indian scarf, bracelets, and hanging copper earrings (*What the hell did she bring on her trip?*), and admire this woman in the floor-length mirror for a few seconds. She is neither pretty nor ugly. She is not young but then again not old. She is neither thin nor fat. She is me. I am becoming. The doorbell breaks my reverie. I slip on rubber thongs, grab my bag, and Banana and I are off to see Beto and his mysterious wife. It is not until several blocks of our walk that I realize I forgot not only my bra but also my undies. The breezes blow through me.

"I am the air," I announce.

"And we are ..." sings Banana.

"Fabulous," both of us say in unison.

Okay, we're not skipping to Beto's, but this is a close second. It's then when I realize I feel nine years old. It's not that I'm unaware I am, in fact, fifty-five or pretending to be nine. It's just that ... this is how I experienced nine, walking with my *bestest* friend on a small adventure to nowhere. This is my nine-year-old body, subtle, free, almost boyish. This is my curious, playful, attentive nine-year-old mind. This is before I understood I was a girl and all that entailed.

It is my fifty-five-year-old present, the gift of choice. I remember nine, fifteen, twenty-three, forty, forty-seven. They are all hiding in my body and my heart. When I'm with Banana and Beto, I remember twenty-seven and thirty-three. I can slide right in if I allow myself.

The whole idea of being many ages at once opens up my universe. I wonder if Banana, even at twenty-seven, feels the same.

"Sixteen and a half," she responds.

"How the hell do you and Beto do that?"

"What?"

"Respond to the questions in my head."

Banana keeps walking at the same pace. Suddenly, she pauses and flashes me a totally bewildered look.

"I don't know."

She lets those words settle inside for a good portion of the walk. Then she speaks but not exactly to me.

"It's like painting."

"What ... seeing inside my head?"

"Uh-huh."

"A painting ..." she begins.

Silence. I may not know what Banana is thinking, but I am smart enough to know she is seeing something and I should keep my mouth shut. I don't need to prod. I just have to let her be. As we walk, I envision a blurry outline of something, splashes of color and two figures. Are they she and I? They are sitting on separate branches of ... a pine tree. Colorful, birdlike.

"Exactly," Banana says.

"Whoa, did I just ..."

"The painting is already there. I see it first, whole, alive. Poof! Magic! And all I do is fill in the ... blinds."

I don't correct her. She is still seeing. Banana is a hummingbird by my side, moving and still, emanating pure joy.

"No, no. I don't just fill it in. I attempt to paint the picture ..."

We come to a complete stop. As we stand in front of Beto's apartment building, Banana turns toward me.

"But each stroke takes me further and at the same time closer to the painting in my mind. Each brush stroke tells me another story, takes me on a different road. Some are familiar. Some I can't even imagine. Each touch of paint to the paper is a guide to the next. I experience the freedom from Vietnam I sought after and at the same time such a powerful tie to my roots, a magnificent pull to my country, my family, my home. And the terror … for a short while, disappears."

Beto opens the door to his building and is standing there wide-eyed and smiling, waiting for Banana to finish. Of course.

Beto kisses us both on each cheek. I never met a man, a human being, before who was pure love. Every tension I've ever had lifts into the atmosphere, and I instantly become lighter. I know that Banana feels it too, because she is smiling ear to ear. As we follow Beto up the stairs, she whispers, "Lucky girl, this wife." I nod.

Before we even get to the door to his apartment, we are engulfed in the aromas of freshly cooked veggies, meats, and spices I have never smelled before.

"Carly and I have made a feast for our friends."

"You cook together?" I can't even imagine it.

"Always!" he exclaims. "Didn't you and Dan?"

A kind of raunchy, mean laugh bursts from my throat. As I try to control it, it gets stuck in the back of my throat and becomes staccato giggles, spitting into the air. The giggles quickly transform into hiccups that won't stop. Banana's features on her face are frozen in one horrified expression. However, Carly, who floats into the room, smiles tenderly. Even in the middle of my little madness, I realize that Beto has, in fact, met his match in love.

Carly guides me to the dining room and gently lowers me into a chair. Out of the corner of my eye, I see Banana shaking her head and raising her shoulders, like *I have no idea where this insane woman came from; she certainly didn't walk in with me.* Beto just laughs. I feel like the crazy aunt no one ever talks about in the family. Carly brings me water and brushes the hair away from my eyes. I'm in love. It's a shame she's taken by my best friend.

I take a few deep breaths in between sips of ice water. I think I am finally calm, until Beto asks if I'm okay. I try to explain myself.

"You see, in my marriage, Dan was always so busy being … He would never …" The hiccups start again.

Now, the entire room is engaged in laughter, even me. I notice something a little odd, but I can't quite put my finger on it. Banana notices too, because she bestows a knowing nod my way. However, I really don't have a clue what we're in agreement about. The truth is I rarely do. Everything about our friendship just is. Everything about us is as different as it could be, and somehow we found each other, sisters in this new life.

Carly lays a brightly colored blanket on the floor and cushions. She signals for all of us to sit. We do so willingly and easily. After we sit, she ritually lays out the appetizers. I can't wait to taste. We all reach out and hum as we eat.

"What is this?" I ask.

"Acarje," she answers and proceeds to tell us, "fried balls of shrimp, onions, and black-eyed peas."

With each new plate that she lays gently on the floor, she names the dish with the ingredient, as if it is a song she sang as a girl, or an old Brazilian myth she is telling. I am enthralled with the food and Carly.

"*Bolinhos de arroz*, fried rice balls similar to hush puppies, made with rice instead of cornmeal … *Empadinhas de palmito …*"

We taste and continue to hum. I don't ever remember humming while I ate.

"These are hearts-of-palm-filled small empanadas. *Coxinha …*"

Now music to our ears.

"Chicken croquettes made to look like drumsticks."

Beto's whole body is an expression of pride, not only proud of his wife but also his country, his life, and his new friends. His dignity engulfs us all. We barely speak as we eat. I don't remember ever having a meal quite like this. Suddenly, I feel so sad. Sad about the life I was living, the kinds of friendships I took on with Daniel, all the meals I cooked without …

"Love," Beto completes my thought. I decide not to be surprised.

"Amazing, how he does that. A truly gifted man, my husband," Carly leisurely adds.

I am caught off guard with that line. When was the last time I actually heard a person compliment someone on the truth of who s/he was, one human being who was amazed at the true nature of another.

"Damn!" Banana yells.

No. Did she hear that? In answer to the unasked, both Beto and Banana rush to the open windows and slam them all shut. We were so busy stuffing ourselves no one noticed the rain.

I turn to the dining room, and there is Carly magically floating in with tea and dessert. No, I swear, this time she is actually floating. Banana and Beto don't seem to notice. I'm waiting for one of Banana's looks that she is presently not giving. However, look or no, there is definitely something otherworldly about Carly, as if she made herself up, as if she gave birth to this person she wanted to be and at the same time was closer to who she really was. She is floating, for God's sake!

"How did you two meet?" I blurt out.

Beto defers to Carly. "You tell the story."

"No, you," she argues slightly.

"Well, shit, someone tell the story," belts Banana.

We've all come to appreciate her cut-to-the-chase honesty. The longer we know her, the more blunt she becomes. It's freeing for all of us.

"Maria, my healer in Brazil …" Beto glances my way.

Banana addresses me. "You know her?"

"We've met once or twice," I reply matter-of-factly.

Banana shoots me a "we'll talk about this later" look. I smile. It is my first one-up on Banana.

"When I was sent to her, I was a mess. I told you"—he addresses me—"it was because I had no direction. But it was more than that. Much more."

Carly strokes Beto's hand.

"Maria knew. She knew it all when she held my hands. I cried— even before we did the herbs, before we fell asleep under the copaiba tree. Before we went herb hunting, she picked up this bark and began to chew, then spit it out. She encouraged me to do the same. It tasted awful, and I never did find out what exactly it was. I couldn't wait to spit it out of my mouth. We did this three times. By the third time, I was able to chew longer. After the final spit, Maria gave me a damp cloth to wipe my gums, which were bleeding. My mouth was full of wintergreen and cinnamon. And I felt this fire down my throat, this energy. I had come to this swift realization that shame not only dampened my spirit but also almost erased it. All of a sudden, I had more energy. Everything within me had been blocked. Shame was a cancer that was growing, taking over my body. The thing is when you live like this, even as a young boy, you don't even realize that there is another path until you actually feel the difference. With this new body, we began to search for herbs and drank her prepared tea. Suddenly, I became so tired. This is not the tired from extreme fatigue but the kind of tired you have after a wonderful full day of activity and your whole body feels at rest and desires sleep. The kind of tired that one knows he will sleep and dream and sleep and dream well. The kind of exhaustion one aches for. Rest … Maria and I are both drowsy, but before we fall into a deep, long sleep, she says, 'You must meet my nephew, Carlit …'"

"You mean her niece," I gently correct him.

Banana shoves her pointed elbow into my upper arm. At the same time, Carly turns and gives me a long bear hug. Two rather strong reactions to a minor correction.

Carly gushes at me, "I love you! Thank you!"

"Was it love at first sight?" I ask, not really knowing how to respond.

"Oh, it was more than that," Carly answers.

Beto interjects, "It was liberation!"

"Do you know the meaning of the name Carly in Portuguese?" Carly sort of asks.

Banana and I shake our heads no in unison.

"Free woman."

"So cool," Banana oozes.

"I am Carly," I call out.

"Me too," seconds Banana.

"And I am Carlo, a free man!" Beto salutes.

We all salute and toast him with our teacups.

Banana and I know a good exit when we see one. We stand up to leave as Carly whispers something in Beto's ear. They walk us to the door, and we cheek kiss ad nausea but with love. Beto says, "In two weeks, Carly is getting her final operation at Mass General, and she wanted me to invite the two of you to celebrate in her hospital room afterward."

I am so confused. "To celeb—"

Banana quickly interjects, "Of course." She grabs my arm and pulls me out the door, again, a little stronger than I would have liked. We leave the building but not without me showing Banana the large red mark, soon to be black and blue, on my wrist. She has the nerve to laugh and keeps laughing.

We walk home not as together as we began. We are having a blowout, major, silent fight. The walk home is arduous and slow. The fog from the downpour is so low and thick we can barely see in front of us. Everything is in slow motion. I am inside a thick white cloud. My mind is ruminating. Carly … the low, deep laughter … the shame … I am gliding now in this soft cloud, cushioned, protected … The nephew is the niece … And suddenly aware … the liberation …

"Oh my," I choke.

Banana laughs again. "Sometimes, you are such an old lady."

"I am," I announce proudly.

Liberation strikes, and I catch it.

Banana and I hug goodbye. None of those kisses for us. Our fight is definitely over. I watch her back as she walks home, and, of course, she knows I am watching. Banana raises her arms in the air, for my benefit, as the fog mythically lifts.

Chapter 7

The Private Detective and Rocky Raccoon

There is a badger in my bed. He yelps, prods, pokes, and scratches the sheets and my legs.

"Stop," I scream with my eyes closed shut. "Go away!"

He is pulling at the sheets. I am naked. The bedroom is a block of ice in the middle of summer. My body is shivering cold and wet. I crawl under the bed. I too am an animal hiding in a fetal position.

"Are you now completely out of your mind?"

Words pierce and gnaw at me like teeth.

I try harder to open my eyes, but they are glued shut. It is exhausting to keep trying, but I do. Why won't they open?

"You should have been institutionalized years ago."

"Shut up and go away. And take the damn badger with you."

"Jewel," the voice says with exaggerated patience, like a ridiculous priest.

"Shut up, shut up, shut up!"

"Act your age," he reprimands.

But what age is that? Am I five, being taken from my parents' apartment only to be told much later that they had died instantly in a car crash? Am I twelve, with my male foster parent offering Tootsie

Rolls to see my tootsie? Am I twenty, just married and in bed alone, with a twenty-nine-year-old husband who spends the first night on the phone in the kitchen? No, I know what age ...

I am fifteen, under a bed, hiding in an abandoned apartment building. The stench of the hollowed-out building, damp floorboards, and mice turds (at least I hope they are mice turds) make me puke, but I push it back in my throat. Someone will find me. Someone always does. Usually the police accompanied by my social worker of the month. Their faces change, their dispositions never. S/he gives me the same look of disgust and great disappointment. "I'm sorry." I am always apologizing. It is bitter cold. I am wet with sweat and am without any semblance of a winter jacket. Though dressed in my flannel pajamas, I am naked. Bruises line my left arm where he held me in his home. S/he doesn't seem to notice or chooses not to notice. I will be returned, not to that foster home (thank God) but to the halfway house, and told this will be my last chance for a real home.

I will not apologize. I will not cry.

"This home is real. This family I made is about love, for the first time. Do you hear me? Love, damn it!"

I take my thumb and forefinger and literally pry my eyes open and crawl back in bed. No badger. Where did it go? And where is Dan? The clock says 4:00 a.m. What? Is time moving backward? Okay, I just need to refocus, get in touch with my breath, and remember what Banana taught me. I breathe. My eyes are slits as I take in the light of the room. I lie silently for a while until I feel the calmness wash over. Then I conjure up every piece of courage and return to my clock: 7:00 a.m. Damn.

I call out for Dan. He doesn't answer. He doesn't criticize. He doesn't.

"The times keep changing on me. I'm losing my mind," I told Banana in her studio last week. So like her, she didn't say I was, and she didn't say I wasn't.

My overtaxed brain is begging for sleep. I no longer hear Dan or feel the badger pulling at me. Instead, I see Banana's smile. I feel her touch. My nails are the color of the rainbow. I fall deeply.

I wake up to the smell of bacon and eggs cooking. I glance at the clock. It's three o'clock in the morning.

"Who the hell is down there in my kitchen?" I scream from my frozen position in the bed.

"Bullshit," comes a return shout from the kitchen. "How quickly we forget. Whose kitchen? Now get the hell down here before our breakfast gets cold."

Adrenalin knocks me to my feet as I run down the stairs, almost tripping several times, and see a kitchen in complete shambles. And orchestrating in the middle of this mess stands Sparrow Last Month Sol This, spatula in hand.

"Clear the table, will you? We have a lot to catch up on," orders Sol This Month, pointing to the kitchen table with her spatula. Dishes and food are piled high on it.

I begin to make my way through the chaos when Sparrow Last / Sol This tells me to hurry or we will eat cold scrambled eggs. I put a rush on it. Actually, I can't wait to tell her the news of all the recent events. However, when we finally sit, she begins a rather long monologue about her life as a detective—well, really a private eye of sorts. I do have my doubts, but it gets so interesting I don't voice them.

Sol This swiftly walks toward me and demands, "Pinch me."

"What?"

"Pinch me. I want to make sure I'm still alive."

I do and admit quietly to myself how this gives me pleasure.

"Ow, that hurt!" she screams.

"Well, you wanted me to."

"You enjoyed that, didn't you?"

I smile.

"And so are you, my dear, alive and smiling. Eat!"

"You sound like the mother I never had."

"I am the mother you never had."

Sol This voraciously eats and speaks at the same time, her open mouth exposing undigested food. "Well, do you want to hear about the case or not?"

I chew first. "Of course I do."

"Could I have a little more enthusiasm? After all, this is about life and death and a life sentence."

"Oh, please, please, pretty please," I tease.

"Well, if you want to hear the story that bad, I suppose I should begin."

I mockingly clap my hands and reply, "Goodie."

She doesn't seem to notice.

I am caught off guard as Sol begins telling her intricate detective story. So, I must admit I miss the beginning and perhaps the middle. A totally animated Sol doesn't seem to notice. I am caught, as I said, off guard … at first by her hair. Suddenly, it is down her back. I mean, almost to her waist. For God's sake, it's only been a few weeks, if that. And the other important detail is her attire. She is no longer wearing her signature flowered shirt, plaid pajama pants, and wild purple polka-dot jacket. Well, the jacket is stuffed in her straw bag. She is dressed in a navy tank top, tailored blue pants, one-inch heels, and even just a touch of, what is that on her face? Damn if it isn't rouge. She is totally appropriate!

Suddenly, she discontinues her story and stares at me. "What?"

"You're so … normal."

She smiles. "This month. Sol is so last month already."

She now has my complete attention, and Normal This Month continues her tale.

"So, I knew something was off, if you know what I mean."

I don't but nod my head anyway.

"I was determined to find out what it was. So, Rocky Raccoon and I return to the scene of the crime in hot pursuit."

"A raccoon?"

"No, no. Rocky Raccoon, my German shepherd."

"Oh, you never told—"

"Well, I wouldn't be much of a detective without him."

"Raccoon is a professional search dog. He was a police dog when he was young and before he lost his right back leg. But that's another story for another month."

Sol More Normal This Month continues her story: "His wife lay in a coma at St. Mary's Hospital. When I first saw him visiting her, I knew there was something off, and I suppose I knew he was the reason she was there. He was too suave, just a little too handsome. He cried enough tears when visiting but left dry-eyed each day. I really couldn't interrogate him because I wasn't asked to be on this case. I volunteered."

She waited for me to respond, but I kept quiet.

"Raccoon and I found ourselves outside his high-rise, just waiting. We're good at that. In fact, one could say it is our specialty. An hour later, his black Lexus pulls out of the parking garage, and we're on our way. We flew up to the fifteenth floor."

"Literally."

"What do you think?" said Normal teasingly.

"I think that you've been watching too much TV on your little vacation with Rocky."

"The perp was an MD. Maybe his name was even Daniel."

Poor dear, a total act of desperation. However, she finally does gain my full attention.

"There was a staircase in their fancy apartment. Can you even imagine that?"

In fact, I could.

"Supposedly, he found her at the bottom of the stairs. He thought that she had tripped and fell, hitting her head on the stairs and floor at the bottom."

"What makes you and Rocky think differently?"

"Ah ... good question."

Silence.

"So, let me get this straight. You are some kind of private investigator, and I am in a coma in St. Mary's Hospital."

"Well, yes and no."

"What the hell is that supposed to mean?"

"It's hard to explain the workings of the mind."

"This is my life you're inferring about, or should I say detecting. This is not a game."

"I know, dear."

"Pinch me. You heard me. Pinch!"

Sparrow Last pinches.

"Ow! So, I'm alive. This is all real."

"Well, of course."

"So, what about this sleuthing story?"

"It's just a case. Sort of."

"You know what? I'm going back to bed. Will you be here when I get up?"

"I'll try."

"I really haven't been sleeping through the night."

"You look peaked."

"Yes."

"Don't worry. I'll clean up the dishes."

"Thanks ... I guess."

I get into my single wrought iron bed and begin to fall asleep. My snoring wakes me, and I see Sol sitting. Her face looks uncharacteristically kind.

"Sleep," she hums.

I drift into a restful sleep only to awaken to a large, three-legged German shepherd at the foot of my bed. As soon as my eyes open, he jumps on my stomach and begins to lick my face. I've just inherited Racoon.

"At least you're no badger," I say out loud.

He kisses my cheeks. It is instant love on this bed between Rocky Racoon and me.

I call Banana to tell her about my new roomie.

"Guess what?"

"Oh no," she squeals.

I keep forgetting about her mind reading.

"What's his name?"

"You mean you don't know?"

Silence.

"Rocky Raccoon."

Pause.

Michelle A. Gabow

"Like the song ..." I say and then sing:

> And now Rocky Raccoon he fell back in his room.
> Only to find Gideon's bible
> Gideon checked out and he left it no doubt
> To help with good Rocky's revival ...

I realize that Banana doesn't know this Beatles tune. Sparrow Last and I are not only from a different country but a different generation. However, she gets right into it.

"I'm coming over to celebrate."

Before Banana hangs up, I confess to her that I believe Sol This is stalking my ex.

"What ex? You're still married to the man," she reminds me.

We hang up, and I stare at Rocky. He is sitting so princely on his three legs. My revival is smiling.

Chapter 8

The Long and Longer Walk

That's what it's like walking with Rocky. Silence. Pure. Fresh silence. Magical silence. From the moment of our first walk or our walk with friends, whether through the busy streets of Jamaica Plain, or back roads, or Franklin Park, Rocky introduced me and then Banana to a quiet we had never known.

Sitting in my bed with this smiling prince in front of me was a completely new way to awaken. His leash and collar were carefully placed on the chair. His tail swishing rhythmically from side to side led me, and I responded.

The First Walk

I call out for Sol This Month. No response. Rocky circles the bed. "It's time. It's time," he silently says. His energy catches me as I quickly dress in a shift and sneaks.

"I'm ready. I'm ready," I say. "Let's go."

Rocky Raccoon, in all his enthusiasm, slowly glides down the stairs. Managing on three legs isn't easy, but he has it down. I witness as he leads with his two back legs and his front leg follows. He doesn't barrel down the stairs but waltzes. We take our time but move forward. There are no voices in my ear, no judgments spewing out of nowhere, no apologies. My mind is blank. And not a bad blank or a frozen blank or a not knowing blank. More like a gleeful emptiness.

Sol This Month is clearly gone again, investigating God knows what without Rocky Raccoon. I slip on his leash. I wonder whether she left dog food but somehow know the inquiry will lead to a negative response. "That is your job," she says without saying.

Rocky Raccoon leads the way as if he is totally familiar with the neighborhood. Maybe he is. The pace is slow and steady. There is no rush, so we move together, experiencing no place to go. I can't remember when I ever walked with no direction. I'm noticing things. Pink and red tulips on the porch of the house to my left, the aroma of cheese steak subs as we turn to our right, the sun warming my nose, even the air. I can feel the air. Rocky's head is up; his back is straight. He's on a mission of no mission. I realize that I'm not only proud of him but also proud to be walking with him. People who pass us—little girls, old men, young, giggly teens—all smile. I smile back. And so does Rocky in his own way.

I feel suddenly strong yet protected. Perhaps that's what strength is. As a woman, I don't remember ever feeling this way. It's strange and new and fun. My back is straight. My head is up. When I allow myself to drift, Rocky pulls me back to the curb. And I think, *He deserves me not to drift.* He deserves me to be present.

Maybe you're assuming, what's the big deal? All you're doing is walking a dog. Yes! I am walking Rocky for the first time. Because he is so much who he is, I am who I am. At this very moment, I am truly experiencing the neighborhood I live in, not talking, feeling new, being present, enjoying my dog. At this very moment, I am in prayer. For someone who shuns religion, prayer is a completely new reality. At this very moment, I am born.

I know what you may be thinking, or at least I know what I would be thinking. *Oh shit. What am I reading? Is this about a born-again Christian? Is this all about how she found God?* And just to put your heart and mind at ease, I am not a born-again, in the strictest sense of the word. But words are only as narrow as we allow them to be. Each time we wake up in the morning, each time some part of us dies, each small change we make, each time we forgive, each time we blink, we experience birth in the next moment. Although we rarely look at life that way, it is a truth. And Rocky, with his three legs and indomitable spirit, is this moment for me.

Not that I have forgiven so easily. I cannot forgive Dan for his lie and how he made me feel. I am unable to forgive myself for staying so long. I refuse to forgive the pious foster parent who molested me at seven years old. I do not forgive my parents for going too fast down the highway when I needed them. As a matter of fact, I will never forgive President Bush and his madman Cheney for creating a thirteen-year war with Iraq for absolutely no reason. All those lives … I am truly a ball of *unforgiveness*.

Rocky lifts his stub to pee. Nothing is easy for him, but he keeps adjusting. No complaints. Tail wagging as if peeing is a gift. He brings me back to here and now as we cross the street to the Bromley Heath Projects and continue our walk. We are circling home. I don't want to overdo his walk. However, I have no idea what overdo actually is for Rocky. I hope to find out.

An older man walking with a cane asks me how Rocky lost his leg. "I believe he lost it in the line of duty. He was a police dog," I respond.

"Me too. Line of duty. Nam," he says and just stands with us for a few seconds in a memory. I realize that maybe he's not such an old man, or most likely, I'm old too. Vietnam was yesterday, wasn't it?

"Damn," he adds, shaking his head and touching my arm. "It's a good thing he has someone who loves him."

A young boy practically crashes into us from the barbershop to our right. He stops just in time. "Can I pet him?" he immediately asks. I say okay and pray that it is. Rocky luxuriates in the pet and licks the young man's face. I admire the boy's haircut silently. He has it shaved on the sides and a great design with arrows in the back, like no matter what direction or road he chooses, it's the right one. Anyway, that's my interpretation. This is a young man who wouldn't ordinarily say hello to a fifty-five-year-old white lady, and I feel excited to meet his acquaintance.

"What's his name?" he inquires. I tell him Rocky Raccoon. "Do you mind if I walk with you both?"

I don't, and the three of us walk in a glorious silence until we hit Connelly Library, where he proceeds to go straight, and I turn down Paul Gore. Before he leaves, he bends to pet Rocky. "Nice meeting you. Hope to see you again, fella." He smiles the most beautiful smile I have ever seen. I realize after he departs that although we weren't properly introduced, it was a magnificent meeting. Maybe next time I'll even get his name.

Rocky and I circle back on Chestnut. Again, Rocky Raccoon resumes his role as leader. I am in his hands. I remember when Banana said just the same thing when I met her. "You are in my hands now." And I smile. First meetings are so powerful. I don't remember my first meeting with Dan, hard as I try. Well, it was more than thirty years ago. I give up.

The tail of Rocky has its own personality. It's like a metronome beating to dance music. It makes me want to move. I think nobody is looking, and I dance a little rhythm to his tail, shaking my butt and moving my unleashed arm. However, someone is watching and laughing loudly on the steps to our home. Banana spreads her arms, and I let Rocky run into them. It's love at first sight.

Chapter 9

The Wedding

"Why on earth did you marry him?" I whisper in her ear.

"Oh come on, you know why," she whispers back.

"I refuse to be your maid of honor."

"You can't refuse. You're already in the dress."

"Fuck the dress."

"Stop behaving like a petulant child. Jesus, you're old enough to be my mother."

"Your grandmother, to be precise."

I can't believe this is happening. But here she is in a pink wedding gown, a long veil, and her normal wig." All her Vietnamese cousins line the aisles. I didn't realize she had so many in the States. The church feels familiar, but I wrack my brain to remember why. Then it hits me like a ton of fuckin' bricks. It's the same church where Dan and I were married thirty years ago. Nothing, and I mean nothing, has changed. Even the same damn pastor. How could that be possible? He hasn't aged one day. Well, of course that can't be him, I tell myself. There is no way this is the same church. The church was all the way in Cleveland, for God's sake. We are in Massachusetts. Damn, if all churches don't look exactly the same.

The organist begins playing. It is a tinny, strange rendition of

"Here Comes the Bride." I'm not even sure if it's really "Here Comes the Bride." Someone (I have no idea who) pushes me, and I make my slow march to the altar.

There he is, the bastard, waiting for her. A smug, winning smile plastered on his face. His hair graying at the temples, the tuxedo soiled and slightly worn from wear. Bastard! How many times has he done this? I'm sick to my stomach.

And then we both turn. She is coming down the aisle. It's all wrong. Everything is wrong. Her walk has this strange skip to it. Her wig almost falls off.

"Beautiful, isn't she, my new bride," he announces with glee.

Before I can help myself, I'm Dustin Hoffman in *The Graduate*. "Noooooo!"

"No, they can't. They just can't."

***

"Just tell me that you're not marrying Dan."

"Dan?" I can see her puzzled mouth searching for a spot to rest, and this is on the phone.

"My ex, Dan."

"Not your ex, at least not yet. What time is it?"

Silence.

"Shit, it's five o'clock in the morning. Don't you ever sleep?"

"Just say it. I'm not marrying Dan."

"I'm not marrying Dan." Banana hangs up.

My bed is soaked. I am a slimy fish rolling around in my own sweat. Rocky glares at me, puzzled, from the floor. I flip around to get the hook out of my head and jump in a cold shower. Choosing not to towel dry, I throw my wet, cool body into a sleeveless shift, slither down the stairs, Rocky Raccoon close behind. We walk out the back of the house.

From the backyard, I can see the sunrise. I am infused with pink-orange light. Rocky is running and limping throughout the yard, happy as a pig in shit. I breathe and raise my arms. Which is the dream? I stand here motionless until the birds sing into focus a simple painting of a bright yellow sun in the sky with an image of the faintest moon tattoo hanging her head in a beautiful bow. The twins know their dance well. I slowly put my arms down, return the bow, call Rocky, and move back into the house.

The kitchen is sparkling clean, a rarity in this house. I ease myself into the red pleather chair at Normal This Month's fifties Formica table. A good long while. Breathing. Beto would say I was meditating. I say that I am practicing laziness now and on a regular basis. Supreme laziness. Divine laziness. This lady, who once lived only to be busy, is becoming quite adept at doing nothing. In fact, I could even say that it has become my specialty. Wouldn't Dan be surprised? Just thinking of him immediately brings up that morning nightmare and rage.

"That bastard!" I yell. "That fuckin' bastard tried to marry my best friend! I guess he's not so gay after all." Is this really me arguing with a dream? But I barely lose a beat before the rage erupts again. " How dare you! For God's sake, she's my best friend. You have nothing to do with this. I am not *in* your territory, nor am I your territory. How dare you steal one of the few things in life that's mine!"

"But ..." exclaims a hoarse and barely audible voice.

Rocky's ears perk up at attention.

"What?"

Sitting across from me on the other torn red pleather chair is Maria, sort of. I say sort of because her features are so soft, almost foggy, as if she isn't really here. Even though this is becoming commonplace in this new life, new house, it is always a total shock. I am comfortable talking to Maria and scared shitless talking to Maria. Living with paradox is against my nature. Well, maybe my old nature.

"But he didn't marry Banana, now did he?" Maria notes in a soft voice.

"Well, that's only because ..."

"Because what?"

"I woke up."

Maria has an ear-to-ear smile and at the same time becomes foggier.

"Don't you dare disappear on me. I have questions. Important questions."

"Ready or not ..." All I can now see are her moving lips. Rocky growls.

"There isn't anyone who is readier than me!"

And poof. I'm talking to absolutely no one. But Rocky. My biggest question at the moment is, how crazy am I? I'm living in a house that's not mine, with a woman who flies in the night, another soon-to-be woman who floats into a room, a healer who appears and disappears at will, and friends who read my mind. My ex-husband who, as Banana suggested, is really not my ex yet has not come to look for me (even though I didn't expect him to). So, which is the dream? Perhaps that's the point. Real and dream have organically (or inorganically) merged. Maybe I'm a committed patient in a mental hospital in an alternate reality on heavy-duty drugs (that wouldn't be beyond Dan), or I'm in a comatose state in a ward somewhere still in Cleveland, as Normal This Month revealed in her recent story. What really happened with Dan? Is this all the workings inside a mind whose wiring got mixed, so now I am living entirely in my right brain? Did I have a stroke? Didn't I read that somewhere about some woman, a scientist, who recaptured her right brain after her stroke? Is none of this real? Does that make my married life more real? Who the hell am I? Where am I?

"Her name was Lola. She was a showgirl ..." rang into my cross-examination. Beto programmed it into my phone, and every time he called, I had to smile.

I answer, "I get down only to get up again."

"I love you too," he replies. "Guess where Carly and I are at this very moment?"

"Not in bed making love, I hope."

"She said not making love, I hope."

I hear Carly's infectious laugh.

"We're always making love, darling," she sings.

I know on many levels this is true. I literally feel my heart suddenly sink. Will I live my life never knowing this?

"Of course it will happen to you. It's happening now," Beto responds … to my thoughts.

"How do … Forget it. Okay, I'll friggin' bite. Where are you and Carly at this very moment?"

"You have such a sweet slut mouth."

I let loose one of those guffaw coughing laughs. Isn't it amazing how feeling can shift moment to moment?

"Yes."

"Did I ask that out loud?"

"No," he responds.

"I thought so."

We're pulling up in front of Brigham and Women right now as we speak. Our first appointment with the doctor."

"Is Carly really going to …" I try to think of the word Banana used. "To …"

"Transition … absolutely!"

"You know that whenever you need me, I'll be there."

"You are here. We feel your presence, along with Maria's."

"But, Beto, is all this real?"

"You can't get realer. Oh God, Jewel, we're so excited."

Then silence.

"See you," I say to no one.

I put my phone on the kitchen table and stare at it, as if someone will call me back any second, but nothing—no lights, no music, no buzzes. Has this cell phone become my only connection to the real world, the world where healers don't fade into existence and nonexistence with helpful and elusive words? The kitchen no longer feels cozy but cavernous. This whole house is too big for me, too big for one woman and a dog. I am a dot. Is this how June A Few Months Ago felt? Is that why she invited me to live here? Suddenly, I begin to choke. When I realize that I'm actually choking back tears, I let go. Tears flood down my cheeks; snot runs down my lips, tasting of salt and coffee. The choking stops. I am hiccupping, crying, and wailing at the same time. Breathing is more and more difficult. I cough out the words, "I am alone!"

I feel hands on my hands, holding them together. Tightly and gently. Then I feel a kiss on my fingers. "You are not alone."

When I look up, I see a familiar face, blurry though the tears.

"I am here," whispers Banana.

She grabs me from behind in one giant bear hug. The kind of mother warmth I always wanted but never received.

Banana's next words brush my shoulder. "You are my Jewel." The hairs of my neck stand at attention, electrified by her lips, her words. I hold her fingertips close to my breast and lean into her. I have never leaned into anyone or anything like this before.

"I could stay this way forever." I did not give words permission to escape. "What the hell is happening?" That is definitely my own question. My fear. My need to run as fast as I can.

Banana responds by stiffening her right leg. It penetrates my crotch. I dig in harder. "Harder!" I scream. She obeys while kissing my neck. Her kisses are both tender and charged, making my insides squirm. The guardians of my inside secrets vanish. There is no separation between inside and outside. Her nipples barely brush my back, her fingertips circle my breasts and pinch my right nipple. Both of my nipples swell, grow, and rise in her hands. She scratches my neck. It hurts my skin and my heart. I feel the pain from my toes to the top of my crown. It forces me to tremble. I can't stop trembling.

I am wet and on fire. I turn toward Banana, straddling her on the chair. I yank her hair and tighten my hold, pulling her head back past the edge of the chair. I want to punish her. Her beautiful, long neck bends back. I could choke her. Our clitorises join through my wet panties. They are big and juicy and rising. Her eyes lance my soul. Her tongue slivers over my cheeks, like a snake, deep, pungent, and piercing. I am being suffocated by her saliva and scratched by her tongue, which has turned into sandpaper. I can't catch my breath. It is too damn painful. I slap her face. She releases a guttural yell and bites me, hard and callously. She doesn't release her bite. It stings and pleases and liberates. I don't know this me, this wild animal, who is howling and writhing. I come again and again. I keep coming. There is no beginning. There is no end.

I am on fire. The heat is almost unbearable. We rip off our clothes. My whole body gyrates, heaves, and rises as we make love on the kitchen chair. I can't get enough. It's too much. I can't get enough.

Chapter 10

The Dream Is Dead

October 14

Is the dream dead? Or was it dead at birth? When does a dream get born anyway? Are we really responsible for our own dreams? Is there a difference between living the dream you had as a child and living the dream period? After all, Dan was the embodiment of all my childhood hopes. A sprawling home with me as the beautiful wife was the manifestation. I had it all, didn't I? I evolved into designer clothes and smiles dancing happily off the pages of magazines.

I easily blamed Dan for my fortunate misfortune. But we were the victims of the same dream, the one that dictated that being ourselves was dangerous. And it was. It is. Wonderfully dangerous. Provocative. Energizing.

We were all unschooled in living our lives. We didn't understand that books are knowledge not only of the mind but of the heart. Damn, we were stupid. Educated and stupid. That paradox is unforgiving. And not only to those living it. The world suffers from our stupidity. What we think is important can be cataclysmic. We have no idea what can rise from our own ashes. Because the tainted dream deadens our souls. We are angry and don't know why. We long for things we don't have. We are depressed and are told it's something in our DNA. We believe in false gods and saviors. When does the manipulated dream become collective insanity?

I tore myself out of my own life. Surprisingly. Painfully. Change shook my soul and claimed my heart. Who am I now? I am here in my stained sailboat journal. I feel crazy love for my best friend, twenty years my junior. Today is my birthday. Reading fiction shifted my reality. I live somewhere between magic and madness.

Where am I going? Fuck if I know.

We

Sweet, crazy conversations full of half sentences,
daydreams and misunderstandings more thrilling
than understanding could ever be.
—Toni Morrison, *Beloved*

Preface to We

We rise and fall to each other. We break and heal. We are always in touch. Kissing, stroking, holding, telling stories with our hands and bodies, making love with our whole selves. We are the queens of a single wrought iron bed.

Sometimes it is as passionate as our first, as painful, as lustful, as angry. We are gathering our stories, our hurts and losses, and breaking them open. Sometimes it's pure joy and laughter, a metamorphosis of friendship. Sometimes it is an eternal tenderness that grows from nothing we have known and everything we are becoming. The conversation has no limits. It rolls off our tongues, our hearts, our bodies.

Perhaps not unique, but definitely a part of us, is the expansion. The breath of we. Friends become family, so too the trees, and Rocky Raccoon (our three-legged dog), the young man who fell in love with Rocky, morning coffee on the porch, the porch, the water we drink, our neighbors, strangers. An old woman's toothless smile is gospel to our spirit. We are falling in love with the whole goddamn human race. The planet is now our fantastically sprawling home, and those who survive and struggle in it carry the weight of our hearts. We are ridiculous. And present. And not secure at all. And too alive for our own good. How long will this last? Who the hell knows? Strangely, that is no longer the point. Is it?

Dialogue 1

Parts of the Puzzle

JEWEL: A good stiff drink would be better.

BANANA: It's eight in the morning.

JEWEL: No. It can't be.

BANANA: The digital world is blinking a strange and powerful truth.

JEWEL: Shit.

BANANA: You have another date?

JEWEL: No.

BANANA: A job?

JEWEL: Someday.

BANANA: Someday is not now.

JEWEL: (*Giggles.*) No. Someday is not now.

BANANA: Hell no. Musk, salt, the sea, sweat … Is that cinnamon? Mmmmmm. If only my paintings had a sense of smell and taste.

JEWEL: Am I your first … your first …

BANANA: Woman lover. (*Laughs.*) No. You think I'm some innocent little Vietnamese chick.

JEWEL: So you are a lesbian?

BANANA: I'm anything I want to be. You taught me that. See how my little tit fits so perfectly into your bosom? We are pieces of the same puzzle. Yes?

JEWEL: Yes.

BANANA: Am I your dream girl?

JEWEL: Fuck no.

BANANA: Well, thanks. What a mouth you have.

JEWEL: Potty mouth?

BANANA: Perfect American idiom. When did your potty mouth come about?

JEWEL: It disappeared for thirty years. Vanished. Poof! I've just regained it. Like I regained myself. It was impossible to dream you. In fact, to be friggin' honest, Daniel was my damn dream. A handsome, professional man who would save me from myself, my life. Who could have thought that our dreams can come from our very own fears as a child? You are the dream I never had. *(Pause.)* How about you, my love? What were your dreams?

BANANA: I had only one dream—to paint.

JEWEL: So you've been living your dream, your passion, all along.

BANANA: Guess so.

JEWEL: I'm a little jealous.

BANANA: Babe, we are loving beyond our dreams, beyond ...

Silence floats in the air.

Dialogue 2

Horror on the Tellie

Speaking on their cell phones.

BETO: Does she know?

BANANA: Not yet.

BETO: You didn't tell her.

BANANA: I thought I'd let her sleep.

BETO: Damn.

BANANA: I know. Should I wake her?

Pause.

BETO: One second … No, Carla, she doesn't know.

BANANA: What did Carla say?

BETO: She said damn.

BANANA: I just can't bear to see her face when she finds out.

CARLA: *(Grabbing the cell.)* We can't bear it now.

BANANA: Holy shit. I think I hear something.

CARLA/BETO: Is that her?

Silence.

BETO: Tell me, is that her?

BANANA: I think it's the television.

BETO: Well, at least …

BANANA/BETO: Oh fuck!

BETO: Carla wants to know the channel.

BANANA: Does it really matter?

BETO: Carla says yes.

A loud sound.

BETO: What's that sound?

BANANA: It's …

From another room …

JEWEL: Oh my God. Oh my God. Oh my God. Oh my God, oh my God, oh my God, oh my God, oh my God …

BETO: Banana … Banana?

BANANA: I need to go to her.

BETO: What a shitty way to wake up.

BANANA: Thanks.

BETO: Take me with you.

JEWEL: Oh my God, oh my God, oh my God.

BETO: Tell her it's a cruel joke. It's not true ... Banana?

JEWEL: Tell me it's a cruel joke. It's not ... Banana?

BANANA: I love you, and I'm here with you. Beto and Carla are here. *(Shows Jewel the phone.)* We can get through this together.

JEWEL: Banana? What the fuck is going on?

BANANA: Honey ... it's true. It's true. I'm so sorry. Donald Trump is our president.

BETO/CARLA/BANANA /JEWEL: Oh my God!

Dialogue 3

A Sea Change

BETO: You brought flowers! Her favorites. Yellow roses. (*Sniffs.*) Mmmmm. (*Calls to the next room.*) They're here.

CARLA: Yeah!

BETO: That crazy woman is cooking up a storm.

JEWEL: Jesus. We should have brought food. Do you think she's doing too much?

BETO: Of course I think it. But it's been two weeks at home, and she's having a ball in that kitchen. We've been cooking and singing together all morning. She adores you both.

Carla hugs both women.

CARLA: Parabéns meus amores!

BANANA: We should be congratulating you.

CARLA: Are you kidding? I love you two together at last!

JEWEL: You look absolutely beautiful. Who the hell looks beautiful after surgery?

CARLA: Muito obrigado. I feel beautiful.

BANANA: How's the recovery?

CARLA: It's been a little painful. Sitting, walking. But *mas graças a Deus*, I didn't get a FFS. I hear that takes more time. This week I'm going to walk to the market, my first mile walk. Let's eat in the kitchen for today. Too hard to get down on the floor.

JEWEL: (*In her mind.*) *She still floats.*

BETO/BANANA: Always.

JEWEL: Damn you two.

All sit down to eat. Silence. Only small sounds of chewing, smacking lips, and mmms during meal. After the meal, Beto collects the dishes, and Carla leaves the room and returns with a bottle of champagne, glasses, and a bulky plastic bag. She pops the bottle and pours.

CARLA: Here's to the women in this room and my beautiful husband.

They toast their glasses. Carla tries to speak but has difficulty speaking.

CARLA: I ... I thought ... that we ... we ...

BETO: Show them the gifts, Carla.

Carla pulls individually wrapped packages from her bag and hands them to each. There is an extra one that she hands to Jewel.

CARLA: This is for January This Month.

They open packages with individually designed, hand-knitted, pink pussy hats.

Dialogue 4

A Mess

JEWEL: Damn! The least you could do is stay in one place.

MARIA: Well, that's no fun.

Rocky Raccoon is twirling in place, stopping to look every now and then, and barking.

JEWEL: You're making the damn dog crazy. And me fucking dizzy.

MARIA: Just trying to find a comfortable spot.

Maria changes (at lightning speed) from outside the kitchen window knocking on the glass, hanging off the ceiling, at the kitchen sink doing dishes, popping her head out of the oven, in the dining room doorway, and finally at the kitchen table.

MARIA: All this change is exhausting.

JEWEL: Me? You? The election, the world?

MARIA: All of the above, damn it! It's difficult to get comfortable.

JEWEL: Maybe comfort isn't the point.

MARIA: My sentiments exactly.

Maria meanders to under the kitchen sink, where she pulls out a bottle of scotch and pours two glasses.

JEWEL: A bit early, don't you think?

MARIA: My time or yours?

JEWEL: It's 11:00 a.m.

MARIA: Midafternoon in Brazil.

JEWEL: What the hell. (*Downs a shot.*) Let's drink to discomfort.

MARIA: (*Wiggles in her chair.*) You can say that again. (*Pours two more glasses.*)

JEWEL: Discomfort has become my life.

MARIA: An adventure. *(Claps her hands as if excited for the show to start.)*

A figure is standing in the kitchen/dining room doorway.

JEWEL: Really? An adventure … if you think making love with a woman who is young enough to be my daughter's daughter if I had a daughter is an—

MARIA: Welcome to the mess.

JEWEL: I don't like messes. I miss my ordered life. I miss … It's just that I don't know if I'm living for the first time or I'm certifiably crazy.

VOICE: (*From doorway.*) The latter. Definitely the latter.

Maria disappears.

JEWEL: Shit! Where did you go?

Rocky barks and turns in circles. Jewel glances around kitchen and checks kitchen cabinets and pantry.

JEWEL: Damn! I know what this looks like. But she was here. Maria was here. She fuckin never says goodbye. She just disappears in the middle …

JANUARY THIS MONTH: Nuh-uh. No way. We can't have two crazies in the same house. That's not the way it works.

JEWEL: She was right in this kitchen.

JANUARY THIS MONTH: *Right.*

JEWEL: She was.

JANUARY THIS MONTH: You win. But I'm sticking around until we clear things up. I may be here awhile.

JEWEL: I'm really fine.

January This Month saunters up the stairs to her bedroom. Midway up the stairs, she turns and gives Jewel a killer Queen Elizabeth wave.

JEWEL: Welcome to the mess.

JANUARY THIS MONTH: *(Calls from upstairs.)* My pleasure.

Dialogue 5

Another Pussy

Heavy footsteps running upstairs.

JEWEL: What the fuck!

BANANA: It's your charge charging up two flights of steps.

DC is in bedroom doorway. Rocky jumps on bed. Both women struggle to pull covers over their naked bodies.

JEWEL: Didn't your grandmother ever teach you to knock? This is our damn bedroom. The key is to the *front* door. So you can walk Rocky. Why the hell are you coming up...

DC: Wow! Pink hair. It's dope, Banana.

Banana pulls the covers over her neck.

BANANA: Thanks?

JEWEL: Again, what the hell are you doing at our bedroom door?

DC: Oh right. *(Holds out an envelope.)* I need you to open this.

JEWEL: You don't have two hands?

DC: And read it.

BANANA: Two eyes?

DC: I'm beggin' you guys.

JEWEL: Gals.

DC: Right. Gals.

JEWEL: Turn around.

Both women slip on long T-shirts. Jewel walks over to DC, grabs the envelope, and opens it.

JEWEL: Banana, do you have any idea where my glasses are?

BANANA: Not a clue. Never do.

Both women search for glasses. Under the covers, in pants pockets, in drawers, and finally under the bed.

DC: Jesus!

BANANA: Ta-da!

Jewel slips reading glasses on and rips open the envelope. She exaggerately clears her throat for a few seconds. Banana laughs.

DC: Oh come on …

JEWEL: "Dear Mr. Carter …" (*Quietly reads letter to herself.*)

DC: Break it to me. I can take it.

JEWEL: "'Dear Mr. Carter,

Congratulations on your admission to Boston University! For nearly two hundred years, BU has proudly welcomed new students, and we are excited for you to be part of this great tradition. As a member of the Class of 2017, you will join a dynamic student community in a place of endless opportunities. BU offers an unparalleled setting for the next chapter of your life ...'"

All scream.

Banana places her pink pussy hat on DC's head.

BANANA: We crown you.

DC's smile warms the room.

JEWEL: Now get the hell out and never grace my bedroom doorway again. Is that understood?

DC: Yes, ma'am. *(Barrels down the stairs with Rocky, leash in mouth following, waving his acceptance letter.)* Damn!

Dialogue 6

Standing in the Doorway

Jewel, Banana, January This Month, Carla, Beto, Rocky, and DC are standing in doorway on Beacon Street, across from the Boston Common.

- One hundred thousand at least.
- Girl, more like two hundred thousand!
- Damn, look at that one.
- Where?
- Which one?
- That … "Keep your paws and your laws off of my pussy."
- Yes!
- That little girl in front of her can't be more than five. "Trump stop being rude; our children are watching. I am the future." (*Screams into the crowd.*) Love it!
  Young girl with sign yells back from the crowd.
- Love your pink hair.
- Me too.
- Tomorrow I'm going to put on my pink wings!
- You have pink wings?
- Of course. They come in all colors. We'll check up in the attic tonight. (*Yells to the crowd.*) Grab him by the Putin!

- *(To the crowd of marchers.)* Support our dreamers!
- That one's dope. Over there. "Girls just want to have fundamental human rights." I'm with that.
- Beto … Beto!
- What?
- Look over there. Don't be obvious.
- A little late for that, don't you think?
- Glance over to my left in the doorway next to us.
- K.
- The older woman with the Beatles sign.
- "You may say that I'm a dreamer, but I'm not the only one"? Great one.
- Not the sign. The woman holding it.
  Beto glances over, and woman waves.
- *(Waves back.)* Hey, that's Maria.
- I know, right? Can anyone else see her?
- I don't know. You want me to ask? Carla?
- No. Don't ask. Why do you think she's here?
- She needs the electricity.
- I suppose she's no different than us.
- Ohhhh, she's different all right.
  Pause. All continue reading the signs at the march ouloud.
- "You have no idea what you unleashed."
- We're unleashing every moment. Ain't we, babe.
- Every moment.
- Here we go. Truth! "Black lives matter, women's rights are human rights, science is real, love is love, vote 2018, kindness is everything."
- *(Screams at woman with sign.)* Damn! You win, baby. You win. Here goes. Hope I do it justice. "I may be a primologist, but I did not want an oragutan as my president. Apologies to the orangutans."
- *(Kisses her on the cheek.)* You defiintely did it justice, my love.
- There, over there, is a line of signs. They're spelling … Dicktator!
  All laugh.

- "Overcome the overcomb."
- "He's stacking the cabinet with fossel fuels."
- "Lock him up."
- "We see the emperor has no clothes, and we're not impressed."
- "I can't believe we still have to protest this crap."
- "We remember."
- "Not today, Satan."
- "I'm scared."

All look at one another in eerie silence.

Dialogue 7

Crab and Eggs

JANUARY LAST MONTH: Strange, isn't it?

JEWEL: What?

JANUARY LAST MONTH: Your unspoken wish has been granted.

JEWEL: Well …

JANUARY LAST MONTH: Oh come on, you're in love. (*Long pause.*) My love is crab. How about you?

JEWEL: Not for breakfast.

JANUARY LAST MONTH: Get over it.

Jewel laughs.

JANUARY LAST MONTH: Where's my favorite pot?

JEWEL: I told you, it's broken.

JANUARY LAST MONTH: Everything's broken. We live a wabi-sabi existence.

JEWEL: You're mumbling. Talk louder!

JANUARY LAST MONTH: Stop shouting at me.

JEWEL: I'm not shouting.

JANUARY LAST MONTH: Everything's broken!

JEWEL: Ya think.

JANUARY LAST MONTH: I know.

JEWEL: Of course.

JANUARY LAST MONTH: But it's okay to be broken. Cracks are our maps.

JEWEL: *(While cooking.)* Do you have a saying for everything?

JANUARY LAST MONTH: Life is a bet.

JEWEL: Oh God help me.

JANUARY LAST MONTH: Loss is gain. Gain is loss. Yes is no. No is yes.

JEWEL: I'm making scrambled eggs for breakfast. Want some?

JANUARY LAST MONTH: Yes.

JEWEL: Is that a yes?

JANUARY LAST MONTH: And then there are times when a yes is simply a yes.

JEWEL: It is very difficult having a conversation with you. You know that, right?

JANUARY LAST MONTH: Noooooo.

Long silence. Eating their crab and egg breakfasst.

JANUARY LAST MONTH: How is Banana?

JEWEL: She's really found her nitch. Banana is working with a group she calls *rad* immigrant artists. I've never seen her so happy.

JANUARY LAST MONTH: Are you?

JEWEL: I haven't found my nitch.

JANUARY LAST MONTH: Well, it's not a wife.

JEWEL: Right.

Silence.

JEWEL: So, what's your name this month?

JANUARY LAST MONTH: It's complicated.

JEWEL: Simplify it.

JANUARY LAST MONTH: Isn't this fun.

JEWEL: What?

JANUARY LAST MONTH: Breakfast. Conversing with my best friend. I never had a best friend before.

JEWEL: I'm your first best—

JANUARY LAST MONTH: February.

JEWEL: Yes, it's February.

JANUARY LAST MONTH: No, I'm February this month. Next month I'll be …

JEWEL: March.

JANUARY LAST MONTH: A quick study. And next?

JEWEL: April.

JANUARY LAST MONTH: A name that is present and simple at the same time. Did you see my favorite cup and saucer? You know, the one with all the colors from Mexico.

JEWEL: It's broken.

JANUARY LAST MONTH: What?

JEWEL: It's broken!

JANUARY LAST MONTH: Stop shouting at me. I'm crazy, not deaf.

JEWEL: I'm not shouting.

Dialogue 8

One Line

Kitchen.

BANANA: *(Takes out a napkin and marker.)* It starts like this. This line. I am not thinking, *What will I paint?* because I just have to follow where this line takes me. And it takes me ... *(Begins to draw.)* To the next and the next and the next. Before I know it, the world I live on the inside and the world I live in on the outside open up.

JEWEL: *(While pouring another two cups of coffee.)* I love that about you.

BANANA: I just have to listen. Like you are.

JEWEL: But I don't create something out of nothing from listening.

BANANA: You created a whole new life for yourself when most people the same age stay in their life, no matter how unhappy it makes them. You created a whole new life for all of us. You're the glue, baby. Anyway, it isn't something out of nothing. Painting is my answer to everything. Remember your minute story. You were so surprised on how long a minute actually was. It was one of your first so-called research questions.

JEWEL: You were the only one that ever appreciated that story of me, the day I set myself free from busy.

BANANA: That's what painting is to me. A freeing of time to timelessness. It's letting go of the boundaries of self. And yet it is all the self is. I am witness. I am participant. Alive in the beauty of Vietnam, the sadness of leaving, the curiousness of my new culture, new life, the mundane, the magical, the anger, the horror, the humor of our world.

JEWEL: Sort of like reading in my life. It widened it.

BANANA: Exactly. My first brushstroke of the morning is my magic carpet. I am traveling. I am connected. I am one with the world. There is no separation.

JEWEL: The current of electricity. One current. Where the hell did I hear that recently?

Jewel rises from her chair to pour more coffee for Banana but instead puts the thermos back on the table.

JEWEL: The current of electricity. It starts just like this. *(Touches Banana's neck.)*

BANANA: Yes.

JEWEL: This line. *(Traces it down her neck.)* I just have to follow where this line takes me. And it takes me ...

BANANA: Yes.

JEWEL: (*Moves her hand down Banana's breast.*) To the next and the next and the next. Before I know it, the world I live on the inside and the world I live in on the outside open up.

BANANA: Damn right!

Dialogue 9

The Distance between Here and There

Phone conversation.

CARLA: An off-the-shoulder, striped, skintight dress or skinny jeans with an oversized T-shirt with Paris handwritten on the front?

JEWEL: Jeans and oversized tee.

CARLA: Purple high heels or red cowboy boots?

JEWEL: The heels would set it off.

CARLA: You are so right.

JEWEL: What the hell am I doing?

CARLA: Helping me get dressed for our lunch date.

JEWEL: She's twenty-six years old.

CARLA: And I'm thirty-five, and you're almost sixty. So?

JEWEL: I'm jealous of my own girlfriend.

CARLA: I live in jealousy. Large silver hoops or small gold ones?

JEWEL: Oversized hoops. Not that kind of jealousy. Okay, it's not only that she is twenty-six years old. But that is a factor. A very important factor. The truth is I'm jealous of her.

CARLA: Whose truth?

JEWEL: My truth.

CARLA: Oh.

JEWEL: Here she is, and I'll say it again, twenty-six years old, and she knows what and who she wants to be in life.

CARLA: She does?

JEWEL: Yes, she does. And so do you. I'm still searching for truth, at almost sixty.

CARLA: Just searching for truth won't do. Won't do at all. You have to wear your truth.

JEWEL: Like you do.

Laughter.

JEWEL: You gals had goals. Even Daniel had goals.

CARLA: That's *so* American. Americans think they need goals and objectives. That's just not healthy.

JEWEL: Goals aren't healthy?

CARLA: They create distance. The distance between here and there is the problem.

Silence.

JEWEL: You're sounding more and more like Maria.

CARLA: Well, she is my great-aunt.

JEWEL: Of course. (*Pause.*) Does she visit you often?

CARLA: Occasionally. She thinks a lot of you.

JEWEL: She does?

CARLA: My aunt makes very few house calls. Scarf or no scarf?

JEWEL: Banana is twenty-six years old for heaven's sake.

CARLA: Do you love her?

JEWEL: Yes but …

CARLA: Scarf or no scarf?

JEWEL: No scarf. How about that chunky silver choker we gave you for your birthing day.

CARLA: Perfect. You've got a knack for this.

JEWEL: (*Sarcastically.*) Great.

CARLA: It is great.

JEWEL: It's leftover from my other life.

CARLA: Really? Well, it's *now*. Wear it, girlfriend. Wear it!

JEWEL: I got the point.

CARLA: Red beret or green army cap?

JEWEL: Army cap.

CARLA: A real rebel. I'll meet you at Wonderspice in ten minutes.

JEWEL: You're dressed?

CARLA: I had the cell on speakerphone.

JEWEL: Wow.

CARLA: All these years, I've lived a double life. Multitasking is *muito fácil*, girlfriend.

Dialogue 10

Stale Cigars and Whiskey

MARIA: Wrong, wrong, wrong, wrong. Have some more whiskey. Don't shake your head. No is never the answer.

JEWEL: You know I talked with your great-niece.

MARIA: Of course I know.

JEWEL: And she says that you make very few house calls.

MARIA: Uh-huh. *(Lights a large cigar she pulls out of her pocket and smokes.)*

JEWEL: Well, I think that says something.

MARIA: You haven't touched your whiskey.

JEWEL: It's early in the morning.

MARIA: In Brazil—

JEWEL: I know, afternoon. *(Downs the shot glass.)* I think that you've come here to be my teacher.

MARIA: Is that so?

JEWEL: Not sure what you're teaching except how to get drunk in the early morning.

MARIA: That's because you are wrong. I am not your teacher. *(Pours another shot.)* Now loosen up.

Jewel drinks a little slower this time.

JEWEL: So, if I'm so wrong, what are these house calls about? You just want to get me plastered?

Maria smiles.

JEWEL: Beto told me when we first met that you thought he was a healer.

MARIA: A wise man. *(Puts her feet on the table and takes a long drag of her cigar.)*

JEWEL: The kitchen stinks of cigar smoke ...

Maria sniffs around her.

JEWEL: Do you think that I'm a healer too?

Maria shrugs her shoulders.

JEWEL: So, why the hell do you keep appearing? And what the hell are you teaching me?

MARIA: I am not your teacher.

JEWEL: All right, then ...

MARIA: (*Puffs her cigar, drinks her whiskey.*) There is no one teacher. There is no such thing as a school of learning. That's just something some white man made up to make money. Greed is not education.

JEWEL: So you're a healer and a communist.

MARIA: I'm everything you are.

JEWEL: What's that supposed to mean?

February and Rocky Raccoon barrel down the stairs. Maria disappears, leaving her half-smoked cigar and whiskey glass.

FEBRUARY: This kitchen stinks.

JEWEL: It's not me.

FEBRUARY: Of course. You are not drinking and smoking that cigar at 8:00 a.m. It's the invisible lady.

JEWEL: Her name is Maria.

FEBRUARY: You need a job.

JEWEL: Miss Never-Worked-A-Day-In-Her-Life tells me I need a job. Anyway, I now have a job cleaning two houses.

FEBRUARY: You're boozing and smoking for breakfast.

JEWEL: Again, Maria.

FEBRUARY: Right. Listen, I'm your *bestie*. God, I always wanted to say that. You need to be a productive member of society.

JEWEL: Like you are.

FEBRUARY: Exactly.

JEWEL: May I remind you again that you don't have a job.

FEBRUARY: Au contraire, mon amie. Au contraire.

JEWEL: Oh right. Are you still a detective?

FEBRUARY: Detective is a metaphor.

JEWEL: You are a goddamn metaphor.

FEBRUARY: What I do is that I visit mental institutions.

JEWEL: Yes, I figured that out.

FEBRUARY: I'm there for the patients. They get me. I get them. My job is a hospital confidante.

JEWEL: The hospital pays you a salary?

FEBRUARY: Of course not. I am and have always been beyond their comprehension.

JEWEL: And beyond mine I must admit.

FEBRUARY: Do you trust me?

JEWEL: Strangely, I do.

FEBRUARY: You need to confront you ex, reclaim yourself, and fly, baby.

JEWEL: I ...

FEBRUARY: Let's have coffee with that whiskey. Where are more glasses?

JEWEL: They're all broken.

FEBRUARY: They're all brown??

JEWEL: All the glasses are cracked!

FEBRUARY: You don't have to scream.

JEWEL: *(Enunciating slowly.) They ... are ... all ... cracked.*

FEBRUARY: The human condition, baby, the human condition.

Dialogue 11

A Hundred and Ten

In Bed.

BANANA: It's true. I swear.

JEWEL: Damn.

BANANA: She did. My great-grandmother lived to 110, and she was the meanest person I ever met. A real bitch. I was crazy about her.

JEWEL: And you're telling me this because …

BANANA: You're a bitch.

JEWEL: Well, thanks?

BANANA: No, no. Bitchy … you have that part down. Probably always had it down even when you were a Mrs.

JEWEL: Still am a Mrs.

BANANA: That's my point.

JEWEL: Whish. Over my head. Your point being …

BANANA: When was the last time you got angry at Dan?

Silence.

BANANA: Right. Or confronted him.

Silence.

BANANA: Right. Or even told him that you were leaving or ever thought of going back and dealing with your relationship.

Silence.

BANANA: Yes, it is. It is my business.

JEWEL: How did you know what the hell I was thinking … Of course.

BANANA: My God. I'm crazy for you. But who are you? A woman without an identity. A brilliant woman cleaning houses because you have no identification. A woman who can barely exist. You have no driver's license or credit card.

JEWEL: That doesn't define me.

BANANA: Bullshit! You think I'm not scared. You think that living in these crazy Drumpf times, I'm sometimes afraid to go to work, to be part of a group of immigrant artists, afraid my work has become too angry.

JEWEL: I respect you.

BANANA: It's friggin time you respected yourself. You owe yourself and Dan a visit. Get your whole life back.

JEWEL: Are you talking to February these days?

BANANA: Of course I am. All this crazy anger you kept bottled up will kill you. It's time.

JEWEL: I'll know when it's time. Only me!

BANANA: Bullshit!

JEWEL: Fuck you!

BANANA: We can only hope.

Dialogue 12

God Is a Dog

Walking down Centre Street in Jamaica Plain.

BETO: It's on all right.

JEWEL: Yep.

BETO: The search for home is always on.

JEWEL: You write it. Banana paints it. And I read it.

BETO: And the girls.

JEWEL: March and Carla live it. There it is. I knew I passed that hole-in-the-wall the other day.

It begins to pour. Beto and Jewel make a run for it. They enter the bookstore already soaking wet.

JEWEL: Shit! Fuck! Shit!

Both laugh.

OWNER: Coming in out of the rain, are we?

JEWEL: No. *(Whispers to Beto.)* Was that sarcastic?

BETO: I never get the innuendos. That's why we're here.

JEWEL: So exciting! Okay. *(Tears the paper in half.)* This is your list, and this is mine.

Bookstore owner is staring at them.

OWNER: Anything I can help you with?

JEWEL: *(To Beto.)* In case you're wondering, that was not-so-veiled sarcasm. *(To owner.)* No, we got this.

BETO: This book has two different writers but the same title.

JEWEL: Oh right. That's any novel by Murakami or Toni Morrison. They're all great.

BETO: Oh. This is some list. Now I understand why I never see you without a book in your hands.

JEWEL: A bookstore changed my life.

BETO: How about this one? The title is unfinished.

JEWEL: Let me see … Oh that is the whole title, *How to Be Both* by Ali Smith. This one is especially for Carla. And make sure you find this, *One Hundred Years of Solitude* by Gabriel Garcia Marquez. Many of the books on your reading list are forms of magic realism.

BETO: What is that exactly?

JEWEL: Remember when you told me when we first met that there is no separation between dream world and so-called real world in Brazilian culture?

BETO: Of course.

JEWEL: Well, these novels are some of the international and American writers who in their heart of hearts know this also.

BETO: Wow!

As they continue to search, an older woman walks into bookstore with cane in one hand and a book in the other.

WOMAN WITH BOOK: Hi. (*Places cane on counter and holds out her left hand to shake.*) I'm Michelle.

The owner shakes her hand lightly but does not share her name.

WOMAN WITH BOOK: This is my book of linked short stories, self-published with Lulu.

She places book on counter, and owner picks it up.

WOMAN WITH BOOK: I've been a community activist and produced playwright living in Jamaica Plain for over forty years. My plays have been produced on small venues here in JP, Boston, San Francisco, and New Mexico.

Owner smiles.

WOMAN WITH BOOK: I'm not what you would call famous but well-known here in the community.

Silence.

WOMAN WITH BOOK: Last week, I was asked to give a reading at the JP Library and Tres Gatos Bookstore and Café. Great attendance. *(Pause.)* Anyway, I recently retired and am very proud of this book, *God Is a Dog (Lost & Found in Paris)*. It's a book of short stories about being present in the moment and how our animals bring us closer to that, even in grief, maybe especially in grief. Most of the stories are written by me, that is until my characters got in the act and wrote their own.

Jewel laughs. Woman acknowledges the laughter.

WOMAN WITH BOOK: I know that you are new to JP, but I thought as a community bookstore, you might want to read it. And if you liked it and thought that it fit with what you are retailing, you might want to sell it on consignment. No money out of your pocket. And you can check with Tres Gatos and On Centre to see how it's doing there. I believe it was sold out several times in both stores. There is also an article about my work in this week's *JP Gazette*.

OWNER: As you see, this bookstore is very small, so it would be difficult, but I will read it and get back to you.

WOMAN WITH BOOK: Thank you so much. As you know, it's hard to get it into bookstores outside of the community when you self-publish, even with Lulu. *(Exuberant.)* Thanks again. I look forward to hearing from you.

Woman gives a small wave to Jewel and Beto and exits bookstore. Beto and Jewel go to counter to purchase books.

JEWEL: The book sounds interesting. Are you going to get back to her?

OWNER: Did you see the binding on it? So thin, a customer won't even be able to read it. Every Tom, Dick, and Harry is publishing now.

JEWEL: Really. It would be great to have a whole section of community writers. Especially ones that are known to the community and have produced work.

OWNER: And that's why you don't own a bookstore. All these older women would be coming in here to sell their little books, and there would be no room for well-written published novels.

BETO: I wouldn't jump to that conclusion.

OWNER: Oh come on. They're a retired joke.

Owner places the book of short stories in a box filled with old papers. Jewel slams her books on the counter. Owner looks at her in shock.

JEWEL: No sale!

OWNER: What?

JEWEL: You just pissed all over my house of worship!

They exit quickly, leaving books on counter and owner with her mouth open.

BETO: No, you did-n't.

Jewel and Beto walk at super speed in a rainstorm down Centre Street before they burst into hysterics, which they are unable to stop until they say goodbye. And even then.

Dialogue 13

Wings

March is meticulously rolling a joint. Jewel is reading the novel, Kitchen, *by Banana Yoshimoto. March licks the cigarette paper, lights, and takes a long toke. Passes the joint. Sarah Vaughn is playing in the background. Very homey scene.*

MARCH: Amazing that you found a novel that bears your lover's name.

Jewel takes a toke and passes it back. This continues to the music. A familiar dance between the two.

MARCH: Wings ...

JEWEL: Yes, I know.

MARCH: Wings ...

JEWEL: Got it the first six times.

MARCH: Wings.

JEWEL: Jesus.

MARCH: Out of all the names, they chose mine. Do you think I'll be famous?

JEWEL: No.

MARCH: You never know.

JEWEL: Yes you do.

MARCH: Excited about the exhibit tomorrow?

JEWEL: Yes, very. I haven't seen some of Banana's paintings and only a few of the other immigrant and refugee artists. So far, they look amazing and brave.

MARCH: And they chose the name I gave them, Wings.

JEWEL: God help all of us.

MARCH: You have to admit …

JEWEL: It's a great name.

March sings along with Sarah.

MARCH: "'What a difference a day makes / Twenty-four little hours brought the sun and the flowers …'"

Jewel joins in.

JEWEL: "'Where there used to be rain.'"

BOTH: "'My yesterday was blue, dear / Today I'm part of you, dear / My lonely nights are through, dear …'"

Return to listening.

JEWEL: I have a question that I need an answer to.

March turns down the music.

MARCH: Shoot.

JEWEL: Okay, here goes. Do you fly?

MARCH: Do you?

JEWEL: In my dreams.

MARCH: Don't we all. I remember flying all over this neighborhood as a kid.

JEWEL: In a dream?

MARCH: All the neighbor children saw me. Some tried and could get up off the ground but struggled to stay up. It came so easy for me. But when they told their parents, they were informed that it was just their imagination. A girl can't fly. The neighbors, children and adults, became frightened of me.

JEWEL: This was in the dream.

MARCH: (*Pondering the question.*) Dreams ... But I continued to fly anyway, every nap, every night. Later ... in a dream, I flew over the Atlantic Ocean. Everybody on this Atlantic cruise ship was looking up at me in awe and disbelief. (*Pause.*) I remember as if it were yesterday.

JEWEL: Avoiding the question.

MARCH: I know you saw my wings. But have you actually seen me fly?

JEWEL: No.

MARCH: So what makes you ask the question?

JEWEL: I heard it. I felt it.

MARCH: Exactly right.

JEWEL: Oh no, are we talking metaphor yet again?

MARCH: Don't be ridiculous. There is no such thing as metaphor.

JEWEL: That's not what you said before.

MARCH: Unless everything is metaphor.

JEWEL: I give up ever trying to get a straight answer from you.

MARCH: Sometimes we just have to give up and give in.

Jewel goes back to reading Kitchen by Banana Yoshomoto.

MARCH: I think I'm going to be famous.

JEWEL: Here we go again. (*Pause.*) For what exactly?

MARCH: Good question.

Long pause.

MARCH: Maybe my institutional work. Maybe for my wings.

JEWEL: Really.

MARCH: Right. No woman ever got famous from her wings.

JEWEL: Is that a metaphor?

March relights the joint, takes an elongated toke, and passes it to Jewel.

Dialogue 14

Opera

MARGARET: Margaret. And yours?

JEWEL: Jewel.

MARGARET: *(Smiles a toothless grin.)* Of course.

JEWEL: Why of course?

MARGARET: *Spare Change?*

JEWEL: Two dollars, right?

MARGARET: You should know. You buy the paper every week.

JEWEL: Didn't think you remembered me.

MARGARET: I have a photographic memory. Needed it when I was an opera singer.

JEWEL: *(With sarcasm that goes over Margaret's head.)* You were an opera singer.

MARGARET: Oh yes. Margaret Mastony. Sang on the *Queen Elizabeth II* cruise ship. Google me.

JEWEL: Really. You're on Google and on cruise ships.

MARGARET: Wrote a book about my life. *Diva Around the World.* You can still purchase it I think. Maybe not. Another lifetime.

JEWEL: How long have you been on the streets?

MARGARET: Seems like forever. How 'bout you?

JEWEL: I'm not … Shit, I guess I am. Maybe that's why I buy this damn paper every week.

MARGARET: Well, you've got March.

JEWEL: You know March.

MARGARET: We're all known to each other.

JEWEL: She always says that she doesn't have any friends.

MARGARET: She lies and doesn't lie.

JEWEL: To know March is to understand that.

Margaret laughs.

MARGARET: You are a jewel to her.

JEWEL: Well, I wouldn't say that.

MARGARET: It's not up to you to say it, is it?

JEWEL: I guess not. How do you know each other?

MARGARET: We all *march* to the same drummer. Get it? (*Laughs.*)

Jewel looks perplexed.

MARGARET: (*Streetsplaining.*) Part of the same clan, my dear. *(Calls to the next woman passing.)* Spare Change?

Jewel knows that the conversation is over and continues her walk down Centre Street.

MARGARET: *(Calls out to her.)* The world isn't listening. But time is. Two moons. Two lives. Two divided by two is your time.

JEWEL: What?

MARGARET: It's *your* time. *Spare Change?* Only two dollars to save a life, lady.

Dialogue 15

We're All Bald
under Our Hair

MARCH: Google her.

JEWEL: So you're a mental health advocate in institutions who isn't paid because no one appreciates your work. Margaret who hawks *Spare Change* outside CVS every morning is a famous opera singer.

MARCH: And you're a partial ex of a well-known, well-connected, filthy rich cardiologist.

JEWEL: Point taken.

MARCH: Merci beaucoup. We all have our stories. She had a brother. He managed her career, stole all her money, and eventually placed her in a home. She trusted him and had nothing left. Simple as that. How easy it is to fall. Not so easy-peazy to blossom. Each of us has our own story, our own tragicomedy. Even you have your story. Maybe we'll read that someday.

JEWEL: Only if Beto writes it.

MARCH: You and I are more alike than you realize.

JEWEL: Maybe.

MARCH: *Absolument.*

JEWEL: I can see a kind of similar pattern.

MARCH: Which is …

JEWEL: Well, I grew older trying to hide myself and did a great job. And you decided at a young age never to hide yourself and did a great job.

MARCH: You think so?

JEWEL: *Absolument.*

MARCH: More café crème, my friend in the mirror.

JEWEL: Yes. (*Sips from a large cup.*) Mmmm. You do make the best coffee. A trick from the hospitals?

MARCH: No, my stay in Paris.

JEWEL: Right. Anyway, Margaret says she's from your clan. I thought you said that you have no friends. What am I missing here?

MARCH: Nothing. Well, a little something.

March pulls off her pink pussy hat. She is completely bald.

JEWEL: Oh my God! Are you okay?

MARCH: Oh, I'm terrific. Just experimenting with freedom.

DC and Rocky Raccoon come barreling into the kitchen. Rocky jumps up on March and licks her profusely while she is awkwardly and quickly putting her pussy hat back on.

DC: Hi … (*Forgets name for this month.*)

JEWEL: March.

DC: Right. Hi, March.

MARCH: Hi. Going upstairs. Help yourself to coffee. Goodbye. I'll be in my room if you need me.

JEWEL: Why would I need you?

MARCH: Just sayin'.

March wiggles her fingers goodbye from the back as she hightails it up the stairs.

DC: How crazy is she?

JEWEL: Not sure. Pretty crazy, I think.

DC: I'm a little scared of her.

JEWEL: The feeling is mutual. She is pretty scared too.

DC: Aren't you a little scared?

JEWEL: No, I'm not. (*Almost to herself.*) Interesting. I spent my life being afraid of women like her.

DC: I think she hates me.

JEWEL: Are you kidding? She would never let anyone she hates take care of Rocky. She loves you. I think you're a little too normal for her. She's been judged by the normals far too long.

DC: I don't judge her. Maybe I do. I've been called many things; too normal has never been one of them. So, I came here for a reason.

JEWEL: Does that involve my reading glasses again?

DC: *(Laughs.)* No.

JEWEL: Good. Because I have no idea where the fuck I put them.

DC: You are the *cursingist* old la ... older person I ever met.

JEWEL: It certainly took me a long while to get back here. Anyway, what do you need ... my younger friend?

DC: So ... well ... It's a small ... well ...

JEWEL: Oh my god! Spit it out.

DC: I need a recommendation from a teacher.

JEWEL: I'm not a teacher.

DC: I know, but you're the closest I have to a teacher. I'll be a freshman at BU, but I want to take a junior course on black activism. I need to have a recommendation to take those classes. You're the one who gave me all those books from the sixties and seventies to read ...

JEWEL: Yeah, old style.

DC: *(Continues.)* On Malcolm and Angela Davis and poetry by Ntozake Shange and novels by James Baldwin and Toni Morrison. You're the one who believed in me. You're the one who helped me with my application. You're the one who really knows me. We got deep love between us.

JEWEL: True, but there are three things wrong with this idea. One being I'm not such a radical, old … er white lady.

DC: I know we have an unlikely friendship, but hey, that's what makes our story interesting.

JEWEL: I haven't gotten to two, three, and four.

DC: The list is growing.

JEWEL: Two: as I said, I'm not a teacher. And three: what you don't understand is that I have no identification. I'm a kind of a runaway.

DC: (*Slightly above a whisper.*) From the law?

JEWEL: No, DC. Nothing like that.

DC: From an abusive husband. I'll kill him. Oh shit! Did you kill him?

JEWEL: No, my husband wasn't abusive, so to speak, and the only killing that took place was in my erasure of him from my mind. Honestly, he was actually a nice guy living in hiding. Suppose we both were. We were choosing to live a divided life. Neither of us liked ourselves. (*To herself.*) Two moons.

DC: And you don't divorce him because …

JEWEL: If one more person asks me that, I'll scream.

DC: Did this dude have any money?

JEWEL: Lots.

DC: You ain't nothing but a fool.

JEWEL: Well, that's the truth.

DC: And my friend. And my mentor. That's it! You could say you were my mentor. Make up a last name or your maiden name and throw in that you were part of a bookstore collective years ago, which is close to true because, as you so often say, books saved your life … They would have trouble checking.

JEWEL: Your sinister mind scares me. I will not do that. But I could be your mentor and friend. We do have an interesting story.

DC kisses her on the cheek.

DC: You're my girl! You know, I never did understand why you took me under your wing.

JEWEL: Is that what you think?

DC: I just got out of a detention home for stealing a car …

JEWEL: Let's get one thing straight. I did not take you under my wing, though I believe more and more in the power of wings. It was definitely a mutual thing. I saw the love in your eyes for Rocky, and fate or maybe magic kept us repeatedly bumping into each other until we just had to obey the universe.

DC: Sure thing. Write that. Man, we're weird but real. I'm off, without the use of wings.

JEWEL: That's what you think.

Dialogue 16

Welcome

A small art gallery in the SOWA district, Boston.

Banana walks to the front and speaks to an audience of standing room only.

BANANA: Welcome to Wings!

Thunderous applause.

BANANA: As many of you who know, I usually don't feel comfortable talking in public. I paint. I paint the life I see, the life I remember, and the life I want to be, off and on the canvas.

Applause.

BANANA: Thank you, but if you could hold your applause, it would be good for now. I have a lot to say, and it is difficult for me to get through this. So … All of us in this show came from hard lives. The details are in the paint, the sculptures, the photography, words, and installations. And of course, our resilience. For most of us, this has been a terrifying journey. And now with our present government, even more terrifying. You will see many experimental styles, collaborations, mediums, and diverse populations, from several countries, as well as beauty, anger, horror, joy, and deep sadness about our present situation. We and our families came here to move forward. Everyone in this room tonight is a dreamer in every sense of the word.

Begin to applaud. Stop in the middle of a clap.

BANANA: Nevertheless, it is a brave act for all of us, audience and the collective of artists, to be here in this room together. I applaud you.

Banana claps, and so does the room.

BANANA: Thank you to The Finger Art Gallery for opening their space to our show. Thank you all for coming on this cold, rainy night in March. I just want to say one more thing before I introduce you to these brave and amazing artists. The name Wings was given to us but my most unique friend who has truly mastered the art of flying. This is our collective goal, vision, and hope.

Applause and sounds from the audience.

BANANA: Enough speechmaking. Let me introduce our next speaker, who will in turn introduce the seven visual artists who are exhibiting their works. Wings is growing every day. Oh right … There will be a panel discussion with this crazy bunch later tonight. But for now, I would like to present my very dear friend, the glorious Brazilian/American performance artist, hairstylist, and poet, Beto Pereira.

JEWEL: What!

CARLA: Surprise!

BETO: Thank you, Banana, an artist who keeps evolving into an energy that we share.

The dreamers can't afford to sit on our ass
or try to pass
Neither can you & you & you
Nos tornamos o que vemos.
We become what we behold.
Man becomes woman, husband becomes wife
We reshape our dreams
School our lives
Seemless
Alive
Courageous
Nos tornamos o que vemos.
We fly in your fascist face.
Redefining the supremacy of race
and place
All of us immigrants
One country indivisable
Nos tornamos o que vemos.
Look up at the fucking sky
Who are these creatures in the air
Defying gravity
repression
regression
death squads, holocausts, poverty, camps,
and now deportation
Look up look up look up
Damn it
Dream with us
And fly.
Nos tornamos o que vemos.
We become what we behold.

Michelle A. Gabow

Dialogue 17

The Good Wife

Late morning. Banana and Jewel are still naked in bed.

JEWEL: I don't know.

BANANA: What!

JEWEL: I don't know.

BANANA: How could you say that? This is a break of lifetime.

JEWEL: For you, maybe.

BANANA: Oh, excuse me. I thought we were us.

JEWEL: We are an us. But … I don't know how to put it … I'm still searching.

BANANA: Great. Search in New York.

JEWEL: I keep telling you, I don't know.

BANANA: That's not good enough.

Jewel pulls the covers over her head.

BANANA: Really?

Silence.

BANANA: (*Strongly pulls the covers down.*) Act like grown-up!

JEWEL: Every time you get angry, you drop articles.

BANANA: What?

JEWEL: You drop articles of speech. The, a, an, on ...

BANANA: Really ... a grammar lesson now? Run, run, run. Pull blankets over damn head, change subject, make jokes ... This really pisses me off big-time. Is this how you dealt with problems in your last relationship?

JEWEL: (*Almost in a whimper.*) No.

BANANA: Who is this woman who whimpers and hides under blankets? Where is the potty mouth I fell in love with?

JEWEL: She spent her whole goddam life being the good wife.

BANANA: Well, you're not the good wife now!

JEWEL: Aren't I?

BANANA: No, damn it. I'm not your damn husband.

JEWEL: No, you're not. But I'm still Jewel.

BANANA: What the hell does that supposed to mean?

JEWEL: I was the wife of a cardiologist and incredibly lost my heart and soul. I became his life. His work. His stories. His friends. A beautifully decorated goddamn phantom.

BANANA: You left that ghost behind. You took a courageous leap of faith. All of us did. I'm asking you to take it with me, the woman who loves you like crazy. There is a life for creativity in New York. A gallery that will support the collective in the Bronx. A school where we can teach art in the community. This is the dream! More than a dream! These are dangerous times. And yes, it's a dangerous move. But what choice do we have? I can't stay here when the dream of change lives there. Do you love me?

JEWEL: Oh, Banana, it hurts my heart that I'm so in love with you.

BANANA: Are you willing to let that go? Damn it, are you willing to let *me* go?

JEWEL: How is this different from following Dan, Dan's dream job, Dan's dream life?

BANANA: I'll tell you how it's fucking different. *I'm not Dan!*

JEWEL: You don't understand. I spent a whole life in hiding.

BANANA: I don't understand! Are you fucking kidding me?

JEWEL: Thirty damn years. I had no idea I was living a thirty-year life as a ghost.

BANANA: Oh, we're back to thirty years again. Back to your obsession with age. Back to your obsession with our ages.

JEWEL: I was living the life of the invisible before you were even five. I can't go back.

BANANA: I don't want you to go back. I never want you to go back.

JEWEL: You are young. Maybe for a while, there is no us, so you and I can grow. It's not the end, damn it! I want you to follow your passion.

BANANA: But you are not only my friend; you are my passion.

JEWEL: Don't you get it? I was living with a man for thirty years before I even noticed that he was not sleeping in the same bed as me. That is some heavy shit. I just began to follow myself a year ago. One damn year in a life of fifty-five. I just don't trust it yet.

BANANA: You don't trust you. Or you don't trust me!

JEWEL: Both. This is the beginning of your life.

BANANA: This is the beginning of your life too. In that way, we are the same age.

JEWEL: No, we're not. You've been doing art since you were a child. You knew your passion. You knew your heart. You saw your gift. You never tried to fit, damnit.

BANANA: That is just stupid. Of course I did. We all do.

JEWEL: But I did it so fucking well that I didn't even know I was doing it. How could I let that happen?

BANANA: So you're going to punish us, punish me!

JEWEL: No, I want you to be free with new friends—and yes, friends your age, artists, and a new life without an albatross hanging around your neck.

BANANA: You are not an albatross! You can do this!

JEWEL: I can't.

BANANA: You won't.

JEWEL: I won't.

Silence.

BANANA: *(Dresses herself before and while speaking.)* You seriously need to work out your shit with Dan. You can't keep running. Call Dan. Face him. Face the truth, damn it. For you. For us.

Silence.

BANANA: So this is it! You're breaking up with me.

JEWEL: No, I just think we … I need some separate time.

BANANA: I want us both to go. But I'll stay. I love you. I'm willing to do anything for you. That's love.

JEWEL: That's not love.

BANANA: So, love is all about you and what you want.

JEWEL: Yes, damn it. For now. For once in my life. Age gives you perspective.

BANANA: What the hell. Only age gives perspective. I have perspective.

JEWEL: No, you don't.

BANANA: A move to New York isn't even a small sacrifice for love. Even somebody with *little perspective* knows that. Relationships are about compromise.

JEWEL: I can't. I won't. I compromised my life.

BANANA: Maybe you don't know what love is. Maybe you never knew.

Banana bangs the bedroom door behind her.

BANANA: *(While running down the steps, heavy-footed.)* You're going to die selfish, old, and alone.

JEWEL: Fuck you!

BANANA: Not a chance, bitch.

Jewel remains in bed.

Dialogue 18

Bedbound

APRIL: So glad you're here. Rocky Raccoon can wait.

DC: What's going on?

APRIL: You must talk to her.

DC: Who? Jewel?

APRIL: Of course Jewel. Who else? She respects you. She thinks I'm just a crazy old bat.

Silence.

APRIL: Which I am, of course. And that's why it should be you. Follow me upstairs.

DC reluctantly follows April.

DC: What's this?

APRIL: Oh this.

DC: Yes, that.

APRIL: So, she won't come out of her room, her bed to be specific. And she won't talk to me. So I prepare small meals and promise I won't bother her. I place the tray outside her bedroom door. When she eats, at least I hope she eats, she puts the empty tray back outside her door.

DC: Don't you think we should call Banana?

APRIL: No, I'm pretty sure that's not a good idea right now. I think they broke up.

DC: What do you mean? They're the best couple I know.

APRIL: Listen, you're gonna have to trust me on this. I only know what I accidentally, of course, heard by the door.

DC knocks on bedroom door.

DC: Jewel? Jewel, it's me, DC. Can you let me in?

No response. April motions for him to keep trying.

DC: I know you're upset. Is it about Banana?

APRIL: *(Whispers.)* No, no. Don't' mention the girlfriend. Never mention the girlfriend.

DC looks at April strangely.

DC: Hey, Jewel, I'm a really good listener. Maybe not as good as you. But won't you let a friend give it a try?

No response.

DC: Let me be there for you like you've been for me.

April gives him a thumbs-up. But still no reply.

DC: Jewel, are you still there?

No response.

DC: Just let April and me know you're okay. We're worried about you.

Silence.

DC: Oh, come on. We love you.

APRIL: For heaven's sake, Jewel. You're acting like a teenager. This is crazy.

DC gives her a look.

APRIL: Well, not normal.

Another look.

APRIL: Okay, okay. Wrong choice of words from me. Just give us a grunt.

Nothing. Silence. Both wait at the door, unable to move for a good ten minutes.

DC: What's that?

APRIL: What?

DC: Whispering?

April puts her ear to the door.

APRIL: (*Still with her ear at the door.*) I'm a little deaf.

DC: (*Also places his ear on the door and whispers to April.*) For fuck's sake. She's talking to herself.

APRIL: I don't hear anything.

DC: We need to break the door down.

APRIL: Not my door.

April kneels down to the floor and places her ear near the crack in the door at the bottom.

DC: We need to help her. Now!

April motions for him to tone it down and continues listening. Suddenly, she breaks out in a smile.

DC: What you grinnin' at?

APRIL: She's having a conversation with Maria.

DC: Who the hell is Maria? And how the fuck did she get in?

APRIL: Yeah, that's what I always say.

DC: What!

APRIL: Shhhh. Time to go.

DC: There isn't anyone in that room with Jewel. Is there?

APRIL: Yes, there is. At least to Jewel.

DC: What's that mean?

APRIL: I told you, it means Maria is there, Jewel's invisible friend.

DC: You really are nuts.

APRIL: Yes, I am. Let's leave them to their private conversation, shall we?

DC: Not goin' anywhere, thank you.

APRIL: I'm asking you to leave, and besides, I won't pay you if Rocky pees all over the house.

DC: That's blackmail. I'm coming back tonight. And if she's not out of the room, I'm breaking the damn door down.

APRIL: It's a deal.

DC walks downstairs.

APRIL: *(With a big grin.)* Not my door.

Dialogue 19

The Gift

JEWEL: Oh shit. I can smell the alcohol from here.

MARIA: All natural herbs.

JEWEL: Bullshit.

MARIA: How can you hear yourself think with all that incessant knocking?

JEWEL: They'll stop soon.

MARIA: Or break the door down.

JEWEL: That would mean April would have to fix it. Never happen. Too damn cheap.

Jewel begins to silently weep.

JEWEL: *(Through her tears.)* Why am I always starting from ground zero?

MARIA: Good question. (*Lights what appears to be a joint.*) Here. (*Takes a hit and passes it.*)

JEWEL: Is that always your answer? No fuckin' thanks. I need clarity.

MARIA: *Precisamente.* Clarity. I make a special mixture of herbs. Take a toke. Breathe in openness.

JEWEL: Open to what?

Maria shrugs.

JEWEL: Give it to me.

Jewel takes a hit. Knocking ceases.

JEWEL: Wow!

The joint is passed back and forth in silence for a few minutes.

JEWEL: Why are you here? Why is it only Beto and I can see you? Why is—

MARIA: I'm dying.

JEWEL: What!

MARIA: I will no longer be in human form.

JEWEL: Oh my God!

MARIA: I may look young for my age. But I will be 102 years old this week. It's time.

JEWEL: I can't deal with another loss in my life.

MARIA: I will always be here. It's your gift.

JEWEL: What's my gift?

MARIA: The ability to see the dead and dying.

JEWEL: That's just plain crazy.

MARIA: Frederick?

Silence.

MARIA: Your mother.

JEWEL: That was—

MARIA: Nancy.

JEWEL: She was dead.

MARIA: No, very ill … a rare form of muscle cancer.

JEWEL: Damn. How the hell do you know all this?

MARIA: I don't always understand my own gift. But I know things.

JEWEL: Are you telling me that I don't accept my gift?

MARIA: That's exactly what I'm telling you.

JEWEL: Is everybody in my life now dying?

MARIA: Oh no, you mustn't believe that. Then again … our time on earth is always shorter than we think. We must all live with life and death. But your gift is something separate.

JEWEL: But what I want to know is ... why did I stay in a bad relationship for over thirty years and end a loving relationship? What is wrong with me?

MARIA: There is nothing new to tell you.

JEWEL: Then why the fuck are you here, in my bed, smelling of too much alcohol?

MARIA: It's not alcohol.

JEWEL: Right. Herbs.

MARIA: *Sim.*

Silence. Jewel takes another long toke.

JEWEL: Can you at least tell me something I can hook onto? I'm lost at sea here. Literally drowning in my fears.

MARIA: That's my point. You are not lost at sea. You're right on course. *(Tokes and ponders.)* With your husband, you tried to force love, so you opened to and became magic and moved on. With your lover, you tried to force time, so you shifted your compass.

JEWEL: Ahh, with Banana, you mean the age difference.

MARIA: No. There is no such thing as age difference in mutual relationships. A stupid, man-made construct. Age and clocks have nothing to do with time, my dear. You know this from your research on the minute.

JEWEL: How do you know about—

MARIA: Time is different for everyone. Therefore, everyone's time is unique. The goal is not to go forward or backward or stagnate but to go deeper into the ocean of time. Allowing yourself on many occasions to be lost at sea.

JEWEL: Well, maybe I'm just so damn tired of being lost. Too damn tired of searching.

MARIA: Right. Stop searching! What are you, some goddamn 1960's hippie? Though I did love those hippies. Their visits kept me busy and on my toes in the sixties and seventies. Too busy. Though they were entertaining and open, I was glad when the numbers withered. Good for me, bad for the universe.

JEWEL: What do I do now?

MARIA: When in doubt, stop.

JEWEL: That's it. Stop?

MARIA: You are the mirror, my dear.

Silence.

MARIA: Now is your time to see the gifts with soft eyes. Soft eyes.

Maria does her evaporation trick and is gone.

JEWEL: Don't leave me now. I need you.

MARIA: *(Just her voice.)* Wrong again.

Maria's laughter penetrates the room. Then silence and the small sounds of Jewel breathing in and out, in and out, in ... And finally, one solitary tear.

JEWEL: Goodbye, my dear, belligerent friend.

Dialogue 20

Birds of a Feather

Two lounge chairs in the backyard, facing a large puddingstone wall, part of the natural geography of Jamaica Plain. May is sitting in one. She is imitating the birdcalls of the crow, blue jay, robin, woodpecker, and cardinal. They are responding in kind. Surround sound in the backyard. Jewel walks out with two cups of coffee, breaks into a large grin in hearing the interchange, sits in the empty chair, and hands a cup to May.

JEWEL: Quite a conversation you have going.

MAY: Birds of a feather.

Both women sit quietly listening to the cacophony around them.

JEWEL: What are they saying?

MAY: (*Smiles and faces Jewel.*) Oh they're just checking to make sure their *besties* are close by.

JEWEL: Interesting. Anything else?

MAY: They have been dreaming of spring so long they're singing it into being.

JEWEL: Amazing.

MAY: Yes, it is.

Pause.

MAY: We are born singing and somehow along the way lose the sound of our own voice.

JEWEL: Such a prophet you are.

MAY: That's not how the world sees me.

JEWEL: I know. Life isn't easy for those who fly.

MAY: Or sing.

JEWEL: Not easy but, take it from me, so much more precious.

MAY: Oh my God!

JEWEL: What!

MAY: What the fuck!

JEWEL: What!

MAY: Look up at that tree (*points*) on top of the puddingstone. Way up there.

JEWEL: (*Places her hand above her eyes to block the sun.*) I see a very large black crow. Damn, it's huge.

MAY: Keep watching.

JEWEL: Do you see what I see?

MAY: The crow is shape-shifting back and forth, back and forth. To an old woman lounging on a branch, smiling.

JEWEL: Damn.

MAY: Holy shit, is that …

JEWEL: Yes.

May rises from her seat and dances around the chairs.

MAY: I wonder why she has suddenly showed herself to me.

JEWEL: I may know the answer to that.

MAY: Well …

JEWEL: I think Maria has passed.

MAY: Passed what?

JEWEL: Her time on earth.

MAY: Oh well, that makes sense. I often see the dead.

JEWEL: We have that in common.

Pause.

JEWEL: I should let Beto and Carla know.

MAY: I get the feeling they already know.

JEWEL: She's the one who introduced them. Perhaps we should plan a service. I never really met her. However, I knew her and was able to say goodbye. More than I was able to do for my own mom and dad.

MAY: Grief is long and hard but changes like the wind. And every now and then, a hello will surprise you.

Silence. Both women close their eyes simultaneously.

MAY: I'll start.

JEWEL: Start what?

MAY: Our service of sorts.

JEWEL: Shouldn't we invite Beto and Carla?

MAY: And Banana ...

JEWEL: Yes, and Banana.

MAY: No, not today. Of course, this will be one of many services. However, Maria appeared to both of us today. Now is priceless. Let's begin.

JEWEL: Again, what?

MAY: Dreaming. Maria helped you begin to live the dream. If we could do anything we desired and not worry about finances for now, how would we live? What is the dream?

JEWEL: I don't know where to begin.

MAY: Like I said, I'll start. Okay, I'd knock down Whole Foods and build a movie theatre.

JEWEL: An independent movies theatre right around the corner.

MAY: Right. We'd have two screens. One only for art films. And the other, only films, good and bad, art and Hollywood, old and new that only have to do with mental illness, so to speak.

JEWEL: Whoa ... cool. But I don't know what this has to do with Maria.

MAY: Look up. She's lovin' it. Now stop avoiding the subject.

JEWEL: Your damn subject. Okay. You and I would spend a year traveling the country, eating and visiting all the really cool café/bookstores and writing a book.

MAY: Two years and all around the world. I'll take the photos.

JEWEL: Titled ... *A Book, a Bistro, a Life.*

MAY: Oh, you're a natural. Love it! We move to New York to set up our own café bookstore and art gallery.

JEWEL: And we'd carry only self-published, well-written books. Community artists could thrive.

MAY: Banana and Wings could show their stuff.

JEWEL: Poets like Beto could read their work. And political discussions and action groups could stretch our minds.

MAY: And the name would be ...

JEWEL/MAY: Wings.

MAY: I can no longer make that happen alone. You know what this means, bestie?

JEWEL: I know.

Both women are silent. The scent of wildflowers. Light pirouetting off dark branches. Splashes of red as cardinals swiftly flutter between trees. Leaves chat. A swish of cars passing on the street. Cotton mists sweep the silken sky, characters of their own stories. A clear, single soprano note of the crow.

Dialogue 21

No Matter What Age

CVS Pharmacy checkout line.

NADINE: Sorry I'm taking so long. First day on the job.

JEWEL: Take your time. I'm in no hurry.

NADINE: Okay. Wow. Shocking blue hair color. Is this for your daughter?

JEWEL: Nope. All for me. I'm lost at sea, so I thought I'd color my hair as metaphor. My way of coloring my world.

NADINE: I know that feeling all too well.

JEWEL: What feeling?

NADINE: Lost at sea. So weird to hear it from an old—

JEWEL: Don't say old lady. Not today.

NADINE: No, I was going to say older person.

JEWEL: Right. The truth is that we have to let ourselves live in lost in order to be found.

Nadine is silent during the transaction.

JEWEL: (*Continues her thought.*) No matter what age.

NADINE: I like that.

JEWEL: Yeah, I'm a real sage today.

Jewel pays for her hair dye and is handed the receipt.

JEWEL: Tomorrow, I'm diving into the wound, so wish me luck.

NADINE: Luck and thank you.

JEWEL: For what?

NADINE: I'm not sure yet.

JEWEL: In that case, you're welcome.

Dialogue 22

Hello

A phone conversation.

JEWEL: Hello.

Long pause.

JEWEL: Hello. This is Jewel finally.

Silence on the other end. Jewel is about to hang up until a gentle voice responds.

DAN: And this is Daniel finally …

You

I would like to end with this thought. That when we reject the single story, when we realize that there is never a single story about any place, we regain a kind of paradise.
—Chimamanda Adichie, TED 2009

Preface to You

"Shit happens." People say that like they're brushing a piece of lint off their shoulders. It's brushed off and shoved down your throat at the same time. Like pain and loss mean nothing. They're really telling you to get over it. Well, how about if you can't get over it. What if it's so deep inside your gut it bloats your stomach. You can taste it with each bite of food. It becomes the air around you. What if you're seventeen years old and shit has become your life.

What if it changes you so much you no longer see the usual reflection of yourself in a store window as you pass. You're living as a ghost. No one wants to be around you. You're contagious. They don't want to get too close, let alone touch. You hear your own mother whisper to a friend that her stepdaughter ain't right. And only you know how true that really is.

Of course, you understand why people begin to avoid you. But it doesn't make the hurt any less piercing. It certainly doesn't make you less lonely. You are brushed away with a flicker of the hand and *shit happens.*

Truth is you can shoo shit away. But it always finds the back door, even if you think it's double locked. There's nothing—and I mean nothing—you can do about it because just when you don't expect it, shit rushes inside. Whoosh ... sadness, loss, pain. If you're a really good actor, you can pretend strong. But that only gets in the way, big-time. You could deny the images or look the other way until you realize there is no other way. Those horrifying pictures play over and over of your dad shrunk down to nothing on his deathbed, or your friend being savagely beaten, or the motherfuckin' clown president telling everyone he could grab any pussy he wants because he's a grotesque, rich white asshole.

And just when you had enough, when you think that you can't stand it anymore, just when you're living as a full-fledged ghost, something grabs onto your father's, friend's, the clown's coattails. For one brief second or seconds, the horror movie stops playing. The cruelty ceases. You notice a full smile on a toothless old woman's face; a soft rain hits your cheeks, and you're washed clean; a bizarre movie takes you to places you never expected to go; a perfectly perfect hot chocolate awaits you on an ice-cream parlor table near a window; the sun sets early, turning the whole damn sky hot pink.

It stops you in your tired tracks. Even though these mini moments feel good, you really don't want them. They interfere with your damn memory. You're petrified you will forget. Who will you be then? But the truth is they can't be ignored. These things that attach to the grief help you to put one foot in front of the other. They help you get up in the morning. They enable you to get a dinner down your throat. For a brief second, they stop the fantasy of ending it all together. You realize in a strange but truthful way that it's the luck of the draw. Whatever tips the scale wins. You know that as long as you live, this "you" is always becoming.

The only thing scarier than *becoming* is the probability that the stepmother is right. You are not all there, whether shit happens or not.

Michelle A. Gabow

April

April 1, 2017
Dear Diary,
My name is Nadine and I am seventeen years...Shit, who am I kidding? I don't have to tell a diary (obviously my first diary) my name. So diary, I think you were a joke gift from my best friend. Or maybe not. All I know is that for months you were lost and then surprisingly you were found. Maybe I'm hoping we're alike in that way. Happy April Fools Day!

April 3, 2017
Dear Diary,
Hope? What's that? My life sucks. Dot High sucks. My body sucks. My step-mom sucks. The clown for president sucks. White people suck. Even my neighborhood sucks. My only friend in the world is missing in action. That sucks most of all.

April 6, 2017
Dear Diary,
I'm so lonely. It's winter cold in April and I'm chilled to the bone. Nothing can warm me up. Nothing. I'm also sick of me. But mostly, I guess I'm just sad. My best friend, S.K. picked you out from a hundred other ugly diaries, no offence. If you knew him, I mean the everyday S.K., you'd have a hole in the middle of the pages you call a heart, like I do. S.K. stands for Some Kid and he was. He is. He had

my back, my heart, my truth. When you're used to having someone around, it's hard to accept absence. He would tell me that's real cold. He would tell me that we got goals together baby girl. He would tell me it's time to get over myself and write, no matter how hard or far or what anybody (meaning my stepmother) says is good or bad for me. No matter! And I think if you really took it under consideration, you'd agree that it's worth a shot.

April 7, 2017
Dear S.K.,
Do you believe in signs? I do. When taking out an old green trash bag with yesterday's leftover pizza and day-old popcorn, the bag broke. Just ripped apart. And out came that funky-ass diary you bought me for my birthday. Obviously, I didn't know it was ever in the plastic bag because I threw last night's garbage right in. But there it was, splayed on the kitchen floor. Your bogus birthday gift with the padded material design of blue-and-white sailboats. Your last joke before you left. Never wrote in it until now. Can't believe that I didn't get the joke at the time. Now, I imagine a wealthy young, very white girl, sitting on her deck, looking out at the water at her father's sailboats, fine blonde hair delicately blowing in the wind. My total opposite. And I laughed so hard. The first laugh, maybe even smile, I had in five months. It's stained with red sauce and pepperoni and stale popcorn butter. I call it my trashy sailboat diary, my joke without you.

Miss you madly,
N
P.S. I'll type this up in the afternoon and email it to you—that is, if you're still at the same address and you can get email.

April 9, 2017
Dear N,
Same address. A social worker here is truly lit and will be helpin' me with the emails if that's cool with you. By the way, there is no life (no joke) without you.

Miss U Madly,
S.K.

April 9, 2017
We're back!

April 19, 2017
That's right, baby girl!

April 20, 2017
But, S.K., you're not here. I can't believe that you're not in my life in person. It's just too damn painful.

April 21, 2017
Dear N,
Yeah, painful as shit. But I'm here and we can make this work. I still believe in us.
Miss U Madly,
S.K.

April 30, 2017
Dear Diary,
On May 26, I will end my life as I know it. In the few months I have left, I will be totally and unforgivably me, and if I'm depressed, so be it. This entry is just for me. There are some things I don't have to share with a friend, even my best friend.

April 31, 2017
Dear Diary,
*Will not expect joy. I will let her surprise me if she decides to.
*I will not try to alter this numb, depressed state. I will not try to change her. I will welcome her just because.
*I will not hate myself for feeling joyless today.
*Today, I will congratulate myself on at least one, maybe more accomplishments.

1. I left the apartment and took a substantial walk. *Yeah!*
2. I filled out a job application. *Yeah!*
3. I returned to this journal. *Yeah!*

*I will not judge myself as not enough (not enough applications, not enough exercise, not enough creativity, not enough water, though I will try to drink at least four full glasses, not enough friends, not pretty enough, not smart enough, not thin enough …).

*I will not admonish the chattering monkeys in my head. I'll let them be. For now …

May

May 2, 2017
Dear Diary,
I got the job! That was fast. Maybe too fast. They must be desperate. Whatever. I will never mention it again in this diary. A job does not define who I am. And who I am is after all who I will become. This journal represents the definition of myself I need in order to survive the way S.K. would want me to, at least for the next month.

May 2, 2017
My dear S.K.,
I got the job! That was fast. Maybe too fast. They must be desperate!
Miss You Madly,
N

May 3, 2017
Not desperate. You're the smartest person I know. Girl, they're lucky.
S.K.

May 3, 2017
Dear S.K.,
I have a question for you. Do you think that we, you and me, are lost at sea?

May 3, 2017
Truth.

May 3, 2017
Aren't we too young?
N

May 4, 2017
We are how we are.
S.K.

May 4, 2017
That's sort of what my first customer said to me today. She said, and I sort of quote, "We have to live in lost in order to be found, no matter what age."

May 4, 2017
Heavy shit at CVS.

May 4, 2017
LOL.

May 6, 2017
Dear S.K.,
The sun is shining in Boston today. I'm sorry you'll miss it. It's warm, not that this would be so exciting in the general scheme of things. But two days ago, it was forty degrees, and today it's eighty. Quite the jump. You'd probably love it because Boston weather emulates and maybe even mocks you in its extremes. This winter was the worst. Bone-chilling. It will never be warm enough to heat my bones. But it's better than rain and grayness and cold and the jolt of losing you.

The month of November has been fucked forever. So, I don't know if you know, but that fuckin moron orange president is now dropping bombs. Remember the night he got elected how we held each other as close as we could get? We knew things would only get worse. And as we both know all too well, they did. I wish the rebel-you could return to Boston to do the wacky, theatrical things you could do against that bad joke. I live with this crazy kind of hope every day. I'll turn around, and there you'll be on your bike, just riding, going nowhere special. A few times, I swear I thought I saw you. One day just staring at my house from across the street. You were wearing your Angela Davis T-shirt. You know, the colorful one that always got a rise out of people. Are you playing tricks on me?

I'm scared every day. In so many ways. On so many levels. We were each other's person. We had our backs. No one has my back. I'm alone. I'm nobody without you.

Today I'm dressed in boy clothes, actually some of your old boy clothes, in celebration of you.

I do daily affirmations now. Don't laugh at me. I hope I'm not becoming my stepmother. Remember how we would laugh at her and her Post-its on the bathroom mirror? God, I am becoming her. Shit! Just maybe it's something she gave me. Maybe she did something right, ya think? Promise you won't laugh. Here they are:
*Today I will remember us.
*Today I'll be anything I please in honor of you.
Miss u madly,
N (not for Nadine but for Nobody)

May 7, 2017
My fabu N (not for Nobody but for Now),
Okay, the affirmation thing is a little weird, but so are you. I never thought your stepmom was as bad as all that. She had her problems, but she did let me stay overnight when necessary, even if she couldn't stand the sight of me. And she provided us with really good laughs, especially when we would dress in her trying-to-be-a sex-feign clothes. I especially liked the red polka-dot miniskirt on me. Girl, I got some legs. And where would we be without her purple lipstick and orange eye shadow? She gave us our secret life. Maybe not so secret in the end, huh?

Are these affirmations really working if you call yourself Nobody? I don't think so. And how many friggin' times do I have to tell you that I am very choosy about my friends? I would and could never be friends with a nobody. So cut the crap. You and Ari are my fam, my only girl friend and my only Jewish friend. Okay, Ari was more than a friend. But in many ways, so were you, just without the great sex. Only kidding. Did you spend Passover with Ari? He has no one there to share it with now. I know you loved him too. Speaking of love and especially of *now* … I got this mad respect for it. Now is really all you have. Everything in the now is spectacular. Your life is a now adventure. An adventure of tastin' and doin' and seein'. Yeah, it's true, and don't I know it. Don't forget it. Never forget it.
Miss U Madly,
S.K.

May 8, 2017
Dear S.K.,
Great to hear from you. Yesterday it was ninety degrees. Today it's forty. And that about sums up my mood swings. So, there's a lot I didn't tell you. After you left, I dropped out of Dot High. The memory of you was just too damn painful. Don't worry, getting my GED at Bridge. My teacher, Ms. Moss (an ex-nun), thinks I should go to college. She seems amazed by me. I like her. Even told her our story. She listened. I mean, really listened. Even shed a few tears. Now whoever heard of a teacher like that?

And, don't faint … I left my stepmother's. No longer in Dorchester, which in itself is really weird. What happened was Ari was *so* sad, as sad as me. We needed each other desperately. So, he is letting me stay on the sofa in his living room. I'm a JP girl now, which I must admit is stranger than you can even imagine, or maybe you can. The other day when I was looking for a job, I passed all these people with signs for Black Lives Matter. They were all white, every single one of them. And they kept smiling and waving for me to join them. I felt *so* obvious, *so* black. Suddenly I really missed Dorchester. I know it's close, but it seemed so far away. Maybe you have to be away from home to see what home could be. Don't get me wrong. I'm really glad they had those signs. But ... Well, just but.

At Dot High, I felt like I didn't belong. Those asses called me uppity. You always said that I wasn't uppity. I was just different. You got difference like nobody else, my friend.

And yes, I celebrated my first Passover with Ari. He's calls it Pesakh. It's really dope. The whole idea. It's about the liberation of the Jewish people from slavery. Don't claim to understand it all, but I can relate to the story. It's our story too. In the middle of the table was the Seder plate that represented the bitterness of slavery, birth, and other things. Ari gave me four questions to ask because I was the youngest at the table. Basically, why is this night different from other nights? By the way, he set a plate for you. Usually Elijah sits there. Then we sang this quirky song, "Dayenu." It means that it would have been enough. In other words, we must fight to keep improving our situation in life. I like that. And then we ate. The whole night was bittersweet because you were there and not there. At the end of the Seder, we both cried. We do that a lot these days. Ari's good folk. I see why you loved him. I love him too.

Miss u madly,

N for Now

P.S. I told Ari that I was writing to you. I kinda skipped that you were writing back. Didn't want to encourage jealousy. He thought it was a good idea but is not ready to do that himself. Ms. Moss also thought it was a good idea. I think so too.

May 9, 2017

Dear S.K.,

I'm new to this email/letter thing. I think I'm supposed to wait for your reply, but I got excited about something. That's so rare these days. Now that I think about it, it's probably no big thing. But it is now. And as you so clearly said, now is what counts. Anyway, this morning in my GED class, Ms. Moss (she now has us call her Debra) began talking about all these horrible bans on refugees and even people that have lived here for years, illegal and legal immigrants, and what is happening to them. How we are all responsible for changing this. How it affects all of us. It was a great conversation. Everybody spoke. Everybody had a story. I felt like we were the United Nations in that class. It was so cool. At first, I was real quiet. Because I wanted to listen. Their stories were horrible and beautiful and painful. Many left not only their homes and families in order to live a safe life. Some lost members of their families on their journey here.

Then I began to blab. I don't know what came over me. You know how I get. I can't stop myself. I asked Debra if you could feel like a refugee in your own country. She wanted me to explain. So, I told her about moving to Jamaica Plain and how different it was. You'd be proud. I gave her a lot of specifics. And she talked about segregation and how Boston was such a segregated city. And yes, Debra said, you can feel like a refugee in your own country. It's all the same fight. After the class, she came up to me and said that I had a brilliant mind. Brilliant mind? Wow. Nobody ever said that before.

Miss u madly,

N for now

May 9, 2017

Dear N for Now,

Okay, I said it. All the time. How easily we forget.

S.K.

May 9, 2017

Sorry. Many times you said it. With you, I was no longer that fat bookworm but somebody with a mind. Somebody who did outrageous things. Somebody. I love you and miss you every day. Today it is raining. The rain cries for me, cries for you. It's so terrible without you. These emails are saving my life. I do not exaggerate.

It's just that I mentioned Debra because the lack of teachers at Dot High who saw me or you. Though they had to work really hard to miss you, especially in Mom's polka-dot miniskirt. They weren't even teachers anymore, just participants in the experiment of testing

and teaching to the computer. I felt we were all being sucked of any fire we had. What the hell was that?
MUM,
Now

May 10, 2017
Ya know, I love you, but, girl, you're taking this now thing a little too far. I mean, your memory is MIA. Off the charts gone. Good thing I still have one. Member how we met? Let me remind you. You were stalking me. True d'at. You followed me to Ms. Hughes's class. Walked right in. Now is the light on? She had the whole class debatin' about *Tale of Two Cities*. Ya know, the best of times, worst of times ... And then this girl in the back raises her hand and begins a whole damn speech about it. About how times were hard even though we were the richest of countries. Then off the rail when you talked about prejudice in our own community. I was a little in awe and felt like you were defendin' me. You were savage, my hero. Ms. Hughes loved what you said and asked if you were in this class. 'Cause no one had ever seen you there before. And you were silent. She said that you were welcome to come back any time. And you did. Ring a bell. Ding-a-ling. Did you ever read the damn book?

Ms. Hughes was fly with her bleached blond, faded Afro and never-endin' personality. And she disappeared the next year. They had admin sittin' in her classes and clockin' her. She was a rebel, like us. Don't know if bein' a rebel is just wantin' to teach real. Don't know if she just left or they got rid of her. Be careful with Debra. Watch out for her because she's buckin' the GED system big-time.
MUM,
S.K.

May 11, 2017
Dear S.K.,
So, I asked Debra if she could get into any trouble teaching. And she said maybe. She said there was a time when intelligent discourse was part of the GED program. No longer. "Teach to the test." That's

their ridiculous motto. I told her about Ms. Hughes and that I was worried. She said because she's been teaching in the system for over thirty years, no one suspects her of real teaching. It's a secret between her students and her. I told her that I want to be a teacher like her. Of course, last week I wanted to be a writer, but I was trying it on for size. She said hopefully by the time I teach, the pendulum would have swung back to progressive teaching and real discourse. Told me that I would be a fabulous teacher. I asked her if there were any books on the kind of teaching she did, and she gave me a list. It's a long list, which is kind of interesting. Do you think any of the teachers from Dot High read these books? Anyway, here are a few of the names: Parker Palmer, bell hooks, Stephen Brookfield, Larry Daloz, Neil Postman. One of the books is titled *Teaching as a Subversive Act*. Kinda cool. Maybe I'll find a bookstore in JP. Debra said that this kind of teaching is teaching to the whole person. I like that. She said these are the kind of teachers we are. Couldn't believe she included me in that sentence!
MUM,
Now

May 12, 2017
Hey Now,
Teach, baby, teach. I believe in you. I always believed in you.
So lonely without you ...
MUM
S.K.

May 13, 2017
My dear S.K.,
Life has no color without you in it on a regular basis. When I get excited about—just about anything, you are always on my mind. What would S.K. do, say, laugh about? What outfit will you surprise me with today? Where is that cackle and snort of a laugh? The only person in the world who thought I was funny. It's the everyday I miss. Holding hands, cutting school, getting baked, dreaming out loud together. Damn ...

Michelle A. Gabow

May 13, 2017
We can still dream together. Don't forget I am with you. Please don't forget …
S.K.

May 14, 2017
Dear S.K.,
I won't. Still searching for a bookstore.
Now

May 15, 2017
How 'bout the library?
S.K.

May 15, 2017
Good idea. Why didn't I think of that? Duh …
Now

May 17, 2017
Hello, my one and only S.K.,
Hope great things are happening up there where you are. By the way, I followed your advice and took out a library card. When I perused (like that word?) the shelves, I finally saw a familiar author on my list. I just pulled the book and took it out. Well, of course it wasn't any one of the books Debra had told me about. But it still was one of the authors, so I began to read it. It's called *Let Your Life Speak* by Parker J. Palmer. I thought that was an interesting title even though I didn't have a clue to what it actually meant. However, on the second page, I found a quote that really spoke to me. I brought it to GED so that Debra and I could discuss it. I waited for her after class. Some other students were also staying late to talk.

When it was finally just the two of us, I told her that I chose the wrong book. But she said, and I quote, "Many times we don't choose books; they choose us." Wow! That whole concept blows my mind. I read her this quote, and I wanted you to read it also.

"The life I am living is not the same as the life that wants to live in me … And I wonder: What am I meant to do? What am I meant to be?"

We talked about that for almost an hour. I think Debra is my first adult best friend. I talked more about you and how you changed my life. Until you, I wasn't really living. And then I started to bawl like a fuckin' baby. Debra just held my hand and let me cry. We sat there for a while in the quiet. Then she began to share her life. When she was in the nunnery, she fell in love with a man and began to sneak him into her dorm. She was white; he was black. They really broke the race thing like you and Ari. You would love Debra. Anyway, she was kicked out, or maybe she left. And now she's this phenomenal teacher. The relationship didn't work, but she began to learn more about her passion and her truth. I think she's the most spiritual person I ever met. I told her that maybe I was learning about my truth, but most of the time I am in the darkness, and I can't seem to get out. She said, and I quote, "Life is a journey through the darkness in order to get to the light. You can't skip it unfortunately." Leaving the life as a nun was very painful and hard and sad, but then she became who she was meant to be. It took time and hard work. And though she is happy, she said that there are always dark times, and we can't avoid them.

When I got back to Ari's, no one was home, and I didn't have to go to CVS (that's where I'm working). It was a gray day and cold, so I lit a candle in the dark room. I just sat for a long time. Sat in the quiet. No music, no TV, no nothing. And for the first time in a long time, I felt whole. I can't explain it. But I felt your presence in me. There was this calmness that I never experienced. It took over me. It was as if I didn't exist, and at the same time I was totally there. It was real cool.

I love you so much. You are the one who made me feel real.
MUM,
Now

May 19, 2017
S.K., I know that I should wait for a response before I write, but I'm so pissed. And I probably wouldn't be pissed if you were around

because we would make everything into a joke. So now I'm pissed at you. I shouldn't be, but I am. This is exactly when a good joke could save a life. I know what you're thinking, *Cut the drama*. So let me tell you the whole story.

It was 4:00 p.m., and I just got out of work. I stopped by J.P. Licks to get a hot chocolate and look out the window. J.P. Licks is practically across the street from my job. One of the bennies. I spent a long time reading Parker Palmer, daydreaming, and making up stories about the people walking by. For the first time in a very long time, I felt happy. I was the me who I always imagined I would be. The hot chocolate was perfection with cinnamon and whipped cream. I took such a long time sipping it that it was ice cold by the time I decided to move on.

I decided not to just walk my usual route down Centre Street to Ari's but to travel down some back streets. And on this tiny street right near where I work was a tiny bookstore, the one I had been searching for. I couldn't believe it. I almost jumped up and clapped my hands, but I used my self-control and just nonchalantly walked in. As soon as I walked in, I felt a vibe, but I ignored it because sometimes, as you well know, I feel vibes that don't exist. As you've often said, I'm *vibration sensitive*. Anyway, I walk in, and there is a thirty-something white woman sitting at a small desk next to the door. She seems nice enough until she asks, "Can I help you?" And it's definitely that kind of help you that really says what the hell are you doing in my store. Again, I try not to notice. "I'm looking for books on education." Her response (with an edge) was, "We only carry fiction." So I say, "Do you have any fiction on education?" That was for you. She says nothing. So I begin to browse and touch every book I pass. Sometimes I pull out a book, any book, and finger through the pages. She is watching, although she is pretending to read a book. Then I drop a few books and say sorry. No response. "Are you sure I can't help you?" she asks but not as a question. "I know what I want, thank you," I say. Then I pretend that maybe I might take one, walk it over to the counter, circle back, and return to a different shelf. I do that twice. I know the truth now. But I can't hide my disappointment.

For God's sake, this is a bookstore. I expect better. Unfortunately, I leave kinda meekly. I hate that about myself. If you were there, we would have fucked that lady up and laughed all the way home to Ari's. But I was on my own. And I'm not as brave on my own. And that's the God's truth.

When I returned home, I felt shitty. I told Ari, and he listened, but really I think you had to be there to see the truth, or maybe it's the black/white thing. I couldn't shake that shitty feeling for days … and the missing of us. So, what started out as a real high became a total rash for days. It's amazing what one bad experience can do, don't you think?
MUM.
N for Nobody

May 19, 2017
Now lapses into Nobody at lightning speed. Breathe, love yourself, baby, and talk to Ari again. This is how you slide. You know it becomes rash the longer it goes on. I know you, my Nadie Now. He is very smart, even for a white guy. He is the best listener. After all, he listened to all my bullshit. Truth.
MUM … Your S.K.

May 20, 2017
Ahh, I haven't been called Nadie in such a long time. It was almost as if you whispered in my ear. I was taken back. Talking to Ari is not as easy as you think. He's as devastated as I am. I sometimes wonder what good either one of us is doing for the other. We never really talk about you anymore. We can't. It's just too much. He works and goes directly to bed. I want to comfort him, but … I dunno. Anyway, I wanted you to see the whole picture.

May 20, 2017
I get it, Nadie. Sometimes I'm a little thick. Maybe I need more exercise or something. Lift weights. Yeah, maybe I just need to lift some weights. I understand. I feel the pain and sadness of losing you

both every minute. No drama there. How about Debra? I bet she'd understand.

May 20, 2017
I wouldn't bet on it, but I suppose it wouldn't hurt to try.
Thanks.
NN for Nadie Now

May 22, 2017
My love … Of course, you were right yet again. You are my best self, and I need to just listen to you sometimes. Don't let your head swell with that one. Okay? As usual, I stayed late after class and after other students. Debra turned to me and asked, "Have you had dinner yet?" When I told her no, she suggested Fajitas and Rita's next door. So we went out to eat, just me and my adult friend, Debra. I felt so grown-up. The food was great. We talked about movies and politics and Parker Palmer. We both just saw this wild film, *Get Out*, and we talked about racism. Over coffee, I worked up the nerve to tell her what had happened at the bookstore. I couldn't believe what came out of her mouth next. "I'd like to punch her in her stupid mouth." I just sat with my own mouth agape. I mean, she's an ex-nun for heaven's sake. But suddenly I burst into laughter. And so did she. I think she even surprised herself. And as we were laughing, I realized that was the joke I desperately needed.

Sometimes you just need somebody to be with you. Two friends laughing at the inexcusable. That's it.
MUM,
NN

May 23, 2017
You go, girl. You're making it real without me. I'm proud of you and, may I add, just a little jealous. How is Ari doing?
MUM,
S.K.

May 23, 2017

I could never make it without you. Get that through your thick skull.
Love,
NN

May 24 2017

Dear S.K.,

Ari is still depressed as hell. What did you expect? I promised myself I would take him out for pizza around the corner, but I don't know, just haven't done it yet. He's not so easy to approach right now, and neither am I, I suppose.

However, I have made two new friends at work. I know, I'm kinda surprised too. Azizi is very special. In the old days, we would say that he's retarded. But he says that he's mentally challenged. And to tell the truth, I'm not so sure about that. He's from Kenya and has this beautiful accent even though he sometimes has trouble getting out words. I looked up his name, and it means precious.

As I said, I don't know how mentally challenged he is. He really is very smart about people. For example, I was waiting on this handsome white dude that was flirting with me, and Azizi whispered in my ear at the cash registrar, "Not a nice man." So, this handsome dude asked me out, right at the cash register, and I told him that I couldn't. Well, he went off right in the middle of CVS. Called me names that I'd rather not repeat. The manager removed him from the store. I was so embarrassed, but the manager told me that something isn't right with him and he knew it wasn't my fault. However, Azizi knew right away. See what I mean? And there's lots more stories like that.

My other new friend is a fifty-year-old white lady named Patty who is missing quite a few teeth but doesn't give a shit. At first, I stayed away from her, but as of late, I love her. She is always telling dirty jokes and has a funny remark for everyone. Plus, she does the best imitations. Patty has Azizi had me in stitches, which makes a boring job so much less boring.

The other day, we all had off of work at the same time, so we decided to meet at J.P. Licks. Well, Patty had me and Azizi laughing so much I almost peed in my pants. And Azizi ran to the bathroom at least four times. We were an odd group, to say the least, and loud, and many people were staring. At one point, Patty gave a guy the finger. See what I mean? She's not afraid of nothing. In that way, and I know this is weird, but she reminds me of you. And Azizi is the kindest person I ever met, and that also reminds me of you. Yes, I'm looking for you in everyone I meet.

Love,

NN

May 25, 2017

Dear NN,

I am touched.

MUM,

S.K.

May 25, 2017

I know, right? Next week, we are all going to the movies. Oh, by the way, Patty never got married. She said that there wasn't any man good enough and she doesn't need "no man" to be happy. Cool, huh?

May 26, 2017

Dear Diary,

Well, you know what day this is. I just have to move it forward a few months. I can't fuck over my movie buddies right now. Nor Debra or my GED, which I will have in September. The new date is September 5. This is our little secret. As I said quite clearly, S.K. doesn't have to know everything.

June

June 5, 2017

Hey Nadie,

Where are you? Missing in action? You okay? I'd like to report news from my life, but nothing really happens here—same old, same old. Girl, I need to hear about you now. Don't make this queen beg. It would just be too damn tragic.

MUM,

S.K.

June 6, 2017

So sorry, S.K. Didn't mean to make you beg (ha ha). But it does touch my heart that you still worry.

MUM,

Nadie

June 7, 2017

Of course I worry, you little shit. What the fuck is happening?

S.K.

June 9, 2017

My own shit just got in the way of letter writing. Been feelin' kinda low these days. No real reason. Well, you not bein' here. But it's more and deeper than that. It's like something scary is buried inside me. This ugly animal. And when she rears her head, I have no control. I can't keep her down. Her growl vibrates inside my head. And I feel this strange meanness in my heart. If I try to squelch it, this bizarre animal sits on my chest. She's heavy, and it hurts like hell. Then, boom, I've exploded. I know that you've seen it. The mean me comes through loud and clear. You used to make me laugh at myself even when I was in the thick of it and brutal to you. I will never forgive myself for that.

Anyway, the other day, I woke up with the blues and a crazy anger raging inside. When Ari came home in the late afternoon from work, he must have sensed something and asked me if I was okay. You know what my damn response was? It was, "Like you fuckin' care." I mean, here's the guy letting me sleep on his sofa for heaven's sake, in his tiny apartment, free of rent, for no reason except he loves that I love you too. I could see he was hurt, and I didn't give a shit. I was a ball of rage and sadness and terror. Terror of what I'll never know. But pure terror.

I pivoted out of the kitchen and just sat on the sofa, seething, thinking of all the things I'm angry at, all the people who devastated the shit out of me and all the conversations I didn't have but plan to have with them in detail. And as I sat there, the same conversations played themselves over and over with ever so slight changes in each, and the devastation list grew to humungous proportions. It began with the phony lady in the bookstore, then my damn stepmother who doesn't have a clue, my real mother who left for a pack of cigarettes when I was six years old (that's it, she just left), all the students who bullied us at Dot High, my dad in his bed looking like Ari's description of Jews in Concentration camps, the orange clown president voted for by the growing number of no longer closeted racists, the people with signs that black lives matter with no idea why, you in that alley bloody and beaten, Ari and his repressed self, the fact that I'm still alive in this shitty world …

And right in the middle of my little parade of horrors, Ari walks in with a pot of tea. I think it was jasmine. He pours a cup for me and a cup for himself. "It's delicious tea," he says and sits on the chair on the opposite side of the room. "Drink," he whispers. So we do, silently. He doesn't ask me questions. We just drink this tea. Then something begins to happen during my second cup. Again, beyond my control. Tears cover my cheeks, my neck, and my shirt. Ari doesn't get up for a tissue; he just drinks his tea. I'm sobbing without sound or words. It's as if the tears have a life and mind of their own. The floodgates are open. My chest expands, making room for an exit. I can breathe again. And then this very weird thing happens. I literally sense the meanness leaving the premises. Really packing her suitcase and traveling to places unknown. Maybe somebody else's chest. I'm still sad, but something lifts. After what seems like hours, but probably only twenty minutes, Ari picks up the empty cups, kisses my forehead, and returns to the kitchen.

I sensed real love from this man, your lover. I saw what an amazing human being he is. He didn't care that I was a bitch; he didn't let that stop him. Suddenly, for a moment, I didn't care either. I just sat and caught my breath, lied down on the sofa, and fell into a deep sleep. You were close by.

That's it. It was really big. It was really small.

June 9, 2017
My Nasty Nadie Now … I'm always close by.
S.K.
P.S. Isn't it time to forgive yourself.

June 11, 2017
"Happy birthday to ya
Happy birthday to ya,
Happy birthday …"
Nadie, my love, do something outrageous as fuck today.
MUM
S.K

June 11, 2017
Guess what I did? Early this afternoon. Don't know what possessed me. Maybe you. Anyway, I needed a real haircut for my birthday. So,

I did my usual walking around the neighborhood of my CVS. And nada. Oh there were hairdressers everywhere, all white women and men. Some with really funky green hair that I liked. But the prices were outrageous. Like sixty bucks for one haircut. Damn ridiculous.

I decided to walk back up Centre Street to Hyde Square near Ari's apartment. And I spot this really toned guy with the sharpest fade and design. So I follow him. I know ... When will I ever learn? He walks into a really cool sub shop, and so do I. I order myself an early-afternoon Cuban sandwich. My first real treat of the day. And leave a few minutes after him, not to be too conspicuous. Then to my amazement, he walks into a barbershop filled with Black and Hispanic brothers. A dream. He does look at me a bit suspiciously or maybe flirtingly. Whatever. Couldn't really tell the difference. Didn't care. He was a means to an end. A good-lookin' means, if I do say so myself. I get this super fade on the sides and picked out on the top.

As I leave, he actually smiles at me. I pretend that I don't see. Don't want to lose my cool. But he is a specimen of masculine I wouldn't mind in my bed. And neither would you.

I walk down to the CVS by Ari's and pick up some electric-green hair dye like the girls in the shops and run it through when I get back to the apartment. I look dope. Wish you could see. I *so* wish you could see the New Nadine.

Get Out is finally showing on On Demand. Ari said we could invite friends to see it. He invited a few of his Harvard buddies. I'm treatin' Patty and Azizi. This should be very interesting.
MUM,
Naughty Nadie

June 11, 2017
Dear Naughty and New,
Still stalkin' (ha-ha). Have a blast watching the movie with your two strange friends and Ari's Harvard. A real dope mix.
MUM,
S.K. (the first person you stalked and don't forget it)

June 15, 2017

Birthday news! It was wild. Ari had some *Harvardites* over, mostly gay, all guys, mostly white, very moneyed, and more than slightly condescending. Actually more like the white people of the town in the movie. I was the only one who already saw it. So, I was real curious about reactions. I told you how wise Azizi is. Well, he kept predicting what was happening before it happened. As soon as he saw the young white female lead, he said, "No good." Nobody could shut him up, and he was right every time. Ari's friends began getting pissed, and Patty laughed so hard she peed in her pants. She says that she does that now more than she cares to admit. Each time there was a funny but tragic scene in the movie, she would be screaming, "Oh shit. Fuck me? Damn. Motherfuckers." We all couldn't help but laugh.

After the film, we had cheese and crackers, hummus, guacamole, wine, strong coffee, birthday cake, and conversation. Very grown-up. Ari can really lay out a fierce table. His buddies love to talk, more like pontificate (like that word? maybe I'll go to Harvard). They had some good things to say. After all, they all studied racism in one form or another. But the real star of the night … wait for it … was Patty.

Patty began her speech, and it was a speech, by saying these words or something like them. I quote her, but I'm not really quoting. "You're all looking at a bona fide racist. Sure you're not surprised. Grew up in Jamaica Plain before it was JP, before it was many colors and flaming gays. My mother, my sister, my older brother (all dead and gone) were racists, my neighborhood was racist, and my elementary and high school most definitely. We hated black people. You all know what we all called them. I won't say it here. I won't say it again. We made fun of the gays. I did the meanest imitations. We thought Harvard was a bunch of pussies. And my favorite movies all had Doris Day in them. I got in a lot of trouble when I was young and was kicked out of high school. I was one of those girls who actually liked learning. It was for shit. Never got a real chance to use this brain of mine. All this to say when the neighborhood started to change, I was pissed. Had a lot of fights. I was and still am tough. Thank God the house belongs to my family, or else I don't know where the hell I'd be living. All this to say,

I hated black people and would have probably joined the KKK if I had the chance. But then this weird thing happened. I mean I'll always be a racist like you guys but ..." (The boys uncomfortably shifted in their seats and were ready to object. But Patty just went on preachin'.)

"I noticed some of the black people moving in at first, before fuckin' gentrification, had a bunch of the same problems and hardships I had. They also got my sense of humor like nobody. The gays ware a fuckin' riot, and they got me. The lezzies were tough, and they got me too. The Puerto Ricans and Dominicans know how to dance. I know, I know, all stereotypes, but in my life, all true. They know how to dance in partners. I love dancing in partners. The Jews, especially the girls, were brazen like me. I just had to shift if I wanted to enjoy life. The love of my life was a black man, but when our child was stillborn, he just left. Fuck him! Fuck 'em all!

And I bet when you Harvard types saw me, you assumed I'm an ignorant bitch." (Again they wanted to object, but she wouldn't let them.) "I mean toothless Patty. I know what you were thinking about all three of us. Assumptions up the wazoo. I get prejudice. I get hate. I get why whites want to feel better than the Blacks, Puerto Ricans, Dominicans, and Muslims. With all that crap shot into my brain like crack, I still let myself see the truth. Truth is hard. Truth confronts every bone in your damn system. Sometimes it's just fucking ugly. Easier to turn away. 'Oh, not me.' But it was me. And me is the one I had to change. You got to start right here, baby, right here." She then grabs both her breasts.

Nobody spoke. I just screamed. "Preach, Patty, preach!" And from then on, both Azizi and I called her Preacher Patty.
MUM,
Nadie

June 20, 2017
Nadie, Nadie ... great story! You should write them down in my sailboat birthday gift.
MUM,
SK

June 23, 2017
Dear SK,
I am. Love you *so* much.

June 28, 2017
Hi … A beautiful morning on Ari's third-floor back porch. A quiet time before my GED class. Amazing to watch the gray sky part and baby blue take over. Amazing to have this silence—no social media, no traffic yet, no TV (stepmother's was on 24/7), no music, just all sorts of birds singing us to awake. Yes, us. I set a cup for you of your favorite, Bustello, because you are most definitely with me this morning. While witnessing our sky, I wrote a sort of crazy poem. It's been a long time since I wrote anything resembling a poem. Here goes …

    Becoming
A turtle with a hole in his shell,
Or is it a cat casually turning her back on me?
A fuzzy ghost with a candle points the way.
Caterpillar dances the jig.
Dog in a perpetual bark.
Cat devil with horns.
Kissing cousins.
Clawed wonder bird.
Dripping old man's white beard.
Bull transforming into a peering baby chick
before my eyes.
A fish blowing smoke.
Greyhound freeing herself from the den
that surrounds her.
A smiling monkey.
Moon with a jagged nose.
Aladdin's lamp with a genie rising from its lip.
A misshapen mouse screaming at his two friends.
An assortment of everything that is and becomes …

clouds.

To you this morning, my friend. Glad you could be here with me.

June 28, 2017
Hey Nadie ... I see it!

June 29, 2017
Five o'clock in the morning. Maybe I'll be a writer and a teacher. Can't sleep. Obviously. My GED class got me all pumped today. I could toss and turn and crash, or I could get the hell up and write. I choose write. So let me set the scene ...

As I said before, my GED is not really a classroom but the United Nations. We got our Africans, Muslims, Roxbury guys, Dorchester girls, Puerto Ricans, Dominicans, Chinese ex-gang members, Chinatown guys and girls, Charlestown folks, and every form of gay you can imagine. There are gays, lesbians, trans, gender queer, butch, gender nonconformist, pansexuals, and much, much more. You fit nearly every one, which is a feat in itself. Needless to say, this room opens sexuality and preference way up. It reminds us all that we can be anything. That the boxes don't work anymore. That our worlds are more open than we can even imagine. You would be a star here in your polka-dotted skirt and your intelligence! There's even a girl here from Dot High. Her name is Sharon. We probably didn't know her because she was not only much older but very shy, and besides, Sharon was Shawn Jones at Dot High. She's kinda cool but really the most femme girl I ever met. I mean she's got it all goin' on—the heels, the hoops, the fingernails, the purple lipstick. And that girl can write the best truth to power shit. Debra makes her share her work with the group first thing before the class begins. She blows my mind. Usually I hate that girly shit, but on her it's fierce. That and the fact that she is a powerful poet who will probably be famous someday. Anyway, I digress. Or maybe I don't.

So, we began talking about race and Black Lives Matter. Debra just let us speak and every now and then would inject something. Amazing how my friend does that. And for some unbelievable reason, we rarely interrupted each other. Well, everybody but me and my big mouth. We talked about supporting this cause and how many young black men have been killed with no consequences. I said that one police officer was charged and of course was a woman. Debra said that was a point worth noting. So noted. We talked about being the other in this country, especially now. We talked personally and intimately in a group how each one of us was affected. With debate, there was lots of storytelling—personal, real stories. I spoke up about how I felt when all these white people with Black Lives Matter signs asked me to join. Most agreed that was weird but how important it is for all of us to support each other. Even I said that it's good to have folks on our side. And I meant it. One girl from Charlestown said all lives matter. Sharon responded by reiterating the facts that many acts of perpetrated violence, like outright murder, especially against young black people, have no consequences. "That's the damn difference," she pronounced. Then the conversation slightly shifted to skyrocketing crimes against gays, Jews, and Blacks since the clown got himself elected. At that point, I had to leave the room. When I returned, my eyes were all bloodshot and swollen, and I was glad nobody asked me what was going on. I just saw your face over and over bloodied by those bastards the day after forty-five was elected.

And then that same girl, Mona, said that white lives matter and the immigrants are taking our jobs. I think I was still reeling from images of you when I interrupted and cried, "Bullshit!" and got in her face. And boom, everybody was yelling at once. Debra interrupted loudly yet calmly. She said she understood why Mona would think that and it took courage for her to speak. See the way she respects everyone, even racists? But ... she said that is an urban myth. She explained about myths and encouraged us all to gather the facts. Gave us all assignments that really have nothing and everything to do with our GED. Said that documented information is all we have to tell the truth, fight the lies, and it's easy to get. And then I thought about Patty and how hard it was for her to face the truth and was sorry about my reaction.

How come we rarely had conversations like this in high school? God I wish you were here. Anyway, lots to think about, and I'm all fired up. Everything is scratchy raw right now, and that's why I can't sleep.

When I got home from school, I told Ari if this was what college was like, I'm ready as shit to go. He said unfortunately that is a very rare experience in college, especially at Harvard. Damn …
MUM,
Nadie

June 30, 2017
Baby girl, ain't you something. Getting educated and all. I'm there with you. Thanks for keepin' me posted.
MUM,
Yeah, maybe I'm that gender noncomformisthomosexualcrossdresser genderbenderqueer guy/gal.

July

July 2, 2017

Dear S.K.,

It's the damn truth. I got *so* many teachers these days. You will always be my first—teacher, mentor, friend. Ari and I had this deep conversation. Mostly he talked. He does that sometimes. But he says we should watch carefully, as the clown takes stage with his antics, all the rights they are taking from us. I'm watching. Patty and Azizi and I are still learning from each other. Sharon, my newest pal, has been bringing in books for me to read. Poetry and fiction. Have you ever heard of *Nappy Edges*? Well, damn if Ntozake Shange ain't tellin' all our stories with poems. I read them out loud. I read them over and over on the back porch. Here's a taste of my favorite poem:

> my father is a retired magician which accounts for my
> irregular behavior everythin comes outta magic hats
> or bottles wit no bottoms & parakeets are as easy to
> get as a couple a rabbits or 3 fifty cent pieces/ 1958
> my daddy retired from magic & took up another trade
> cuz this friend of mine from the 3rd grade asked to be
> made white on the spot what cd any self-respectin
> colored american magician do wit such a outlandish
> request/ cept put all them razzamatazz hocus pocus
> zippity-do-dah thingamajigs away cuz colored chirren
> believin in magic waz becomin politically dangerous

for the race & waznt nobody gonna be made white
on the spot …

And that's just the beginning. Amazing, right! Just reading it over
and over makes me feel whole and strong and alive. Like singing even
though, as you so often pointed out, my singing voice is as flat as it is
passionate. Sharon also brought me the novel *Sula* (Toni Morrison)
to read too. The friendship between Sula and Nel reminds me of us.
That deep friendship that comes in dreams and is realized in life.
We are Sula and Nel. All I want to do with the rest of my life is read
fiction now. There are no lies in these books, all truth, all life giving,
all powerful. Kinda like how my stepmom talks about God.

Then Sharon gave me one of her poems that I will treasure all
my life. I'm copying it for you, so you can see her and feel her.

July 10, 2017

Yesterday was a very weird and awful day. The weirdness began when
Debra took Sharon and me out to lunch, which should have been
great, right? She definitely has favorites. I don't know if that says
so much about Debra but more about how some souls touch each
other. I will always be grateful for you opening up mine. No one ever
wanted to talk about my mother or my dad, until you. It was the first
time I remember actually grieving their loss.

We met at a time when our souls opened as one, as if there was
no skin separating us. How lucky we were, we are.

But Fajita's and Rita's wasn't what it was usually cracked up to be.
In fact, our lunch punctuated what my damn life has been and still is
about! All the learning in the world means crap if everyone in your life,
everyone that you love, gets fucked. So after lunch but before coffee,
Debra tells us she has breast cancer. She says it kind of offhandedly.
I think she said, "I have a little cancer." And I know all too well from
living with my dad that there is no such thing as a little cancer. I can't
speak. Sharon grabs my hand from under the table, but I push it away.
I don't want it. And then there's this buzz. That's all I hear. I think
Sharon and Debra were talking. Not sure. All I hear is *buzz*.

Sharon tells me later Debra has a sub for the class in the next month, and she will try to make it to graduation. I don't want Sharon to tell me anything that will make it real. In fact, I don't want anybody. I'm not going to the damn graduation or back to school. I don't want another damn friend. I'm a jinx, S.K. You know it. I know it. Everyone I love disappears on me. God's honest. My mom, my dad, my aunt, you, and now Debra ... I should have never left you alone that morning. We were just accosted by a crazy *mf.* An eerie, deafening "Star Spangled Banner" was blasted through the neighborhood from his scary Trump-plastered van. He pointed and yelled at us. This was one ugly, vile dude in our face at 8:00 a.m., the morning after our forty-fifth was elected.

You told me that was just the beginning and then asked me to go home and be safe today. "Are you going home?" I tested. You passed the test. "Absolutely," giving me one of your make-the-world-melt toothy smiles. Then adding, "And having sick porno sex with my handsome man wherever and whenever and however we can in that damn apartment—that is until we hold a big mother of a march or they all just die." You put your fine, long, beautiful, black, fuck-you finger up to the sky, looking like my heroine in that purple skirt, roaring like the lioness you were in the middle of Paul Gore, "Die, you motherfuckers!" I laughed. Damn, I friggin' laughed and left you.

September

September 10, 2017

Yeah, as you well know, it's been awhile. Did I jump off the train platform? Did I fall? Or faint? Was it all three? And who the fuck was that woman who jumped in after me?

I woke up twice from this so-called coma. The first was to you. Sitting silently on the chair at the edge of my hospital bed. Just staring but not at me. What were you staring at? Maybe it was the clouds from a view you haven't seen lately. A smiling monkey. Moon with a jagged nose … Suddenly, you turned toward me. Your eyes were glassy and cold.

Were you angry? It jolted me. I wanted to hold you. There were so many questions I wanted to ask. But the words had no connection to sound.

"Don't say a fucking word," you admonished in a scratchy voice that was yours and not yours. "What's your damn hurry, bitch? You think this is some picnic? You're so damn curious about my world now. Well, flash, there is no life after life. No aroma of Ari's sexy morning cup of Bustello or the salivating taste of a big-ass-juicy-hold-no onions-barbeque burger. Fucking is definitely off the agenda. That hysterical rip shit mad friend you were crazy for, well, girlfriend, he's in the past. I am no longer a hysterical woman and don't have a friend in the world who even gets the joke. There is no becoming. Just a faint loneliness and remnants of memory. Every fuckin' thing we loved about life has split the scene. I'm floating here in limbo until I am reborn, hopefully as a big-ass German shepherd bitch." Your raised voice penetrated the room with such forcefulness and, yes, love, that it shook the bed. "I don't want you here, baby girl!"

Then you vanished. I wanted to follow. Didn't believe your bullshit. But you were gone. I felt my heart tear open and beat so loudly that my brain erupted and burst open. "Please," I spit out. "Take me!" My legs jerked as I left my body convulsing in bed.

Someone is choking the life out of my wrist. "Ouch!" A room full of laughter. It wasn't that funny. This is the second awakening. So, let me set the scene for you. Surrounding the hospital bed were members of my family, mostly my new family, that is. Closest to me, squeezing the life out of my wrist, was Tamika, my stepmom. Tamika's eyes were red, and her skin blotched. Get this. She was wearing not a drop of makeup, not even her signature purple lipstick. Her hair was a short, unkept, unpicked Afro. I don't think I ever saw this hairdo or this face. Where the hell were all of her damn wigs? And then the face came back to me. A face ravaged with grief was how she looked when Dad died. Suddenly I remembered what I had purposely hidden from myself. Her words to me ... "You're mine, and I will love you no matter what. You hear me?" And I realized even though she is my total opposite and felt, maybe rightly so, I wasn't all there, this woman loved me. It was me who tormented her, who blamed her for all my losses, who ridiculed how she looked and acted. It was me who separated us. As I burst into tears, she held my hand securely in hers, not saying a word.

On the other hand, to her left was Sharon. She was made up like she was going to a party, batting those long false lashes a mile a minute. "Girl," she teased with an extra bat, "you had us all worried." Though to tell God's truth, she didn't look too worried. I suppose she looked relieved. And that was enough.

Then there was the shadow that wasn't sitting at all. But walking back and forth, moving arms every which way, muttering. He was moving so fast that his body was a blur, but as soon as I heard his voice, I knew it was Azizi. And in this strange but wonderful way, I felt seen, really seen. "She's the best, coming back to CVS, better beware, Nadie's here, not there, that's the truth, better beware, she's here, not there, and doing her best to come back to CVS ..." OMG, Azizi was rapping.

Sharon rose immediately from her chair in her three-inch heels and picked him up off the floor and hugged him. "A poet after my own heart!" she sang. Did I mention that Sharon is six two?

The room, including me, broke into laughter.

Patty was on my right, her arm shaking my right thigh and mumbling, "My sister, my sister." I saw Tamika give her one of those looks that said sister-my-ass. But I knew differently. I knew how long it took her to be here.

I felt a presence closest to me on my right, but it hurt like hell to turn my head. Finally, my stepmother gently moved my head to the right, and I saw Debra, with little wisps of hair and flat as a board but exuding tons of energy. She was alive and as vibrant as ever. She placed a book in my hand, and I brought it up to eye level, which, may I add, wasn't easy. It was a book by Mark Nepo, but the title said it all ... *The Book of Awakening*. And I looked directly into Debra's blue eyes and barely whispered, "Thank you." Her smile lit my whole body. I broke into a sweat and suddenly felt a wet bed underneath me. I actually had a memory of being born, true and as clear as day. I had been given birth again, from and in this circle. Crazy, huh?

At that point, Ari came rushing in like the rabbit in Alice, late for a date. He yelled, "Nadie, Nadie, you're up." I added as an aside, "And alive." He was clutching your blue-and-white sailboat journal to his chest, which scared the shit out of me. I knew he had suspicions I was unstable. Now he had the proof. I had told him I was writing letters to you, but I kinda skipped that part where you wrote me back. I am your certified split-personality schizo. Ari had the confession in writing, right in his very own hands and close to his chest. He zoomed into my face, kissed my cheek, and whispered in my ear, "Thanks for keeping him alive," and placed the diary on top of *The Awakening* on top of my chest. So much symbolism was difficult for me to digest right then. All I know is that I decided to keep our little hospital visitation and our conversation about your rebirth to myself. That late-night surprise date might have put Ari over the edge. Right?

September 10, 2017
Right … my baby girl. True d'at … we all are being reborn.

September 10, 2017
But why does it have to hurt so much …

September 11, 2017
?

September 13, 2017
My dear friend,
I've noticed that when I give up goals in life, like happy or hopeful, and accept what is, I do a little better. The important thing is what I'm doing right now—writing. For these few minutes a day, I am at peace. I hear music. I enter another world. The world of us and I can breathe again. This is my own pill for depression, for anger, for anxiety. It doesn't make it go away but enlarges what is imaginable somehow.

Thank you for making this world possible. Thank you for my outrageously ugly journal.

September 13, 2017
You're welcome, Nadie.

September 20, 2017
There isn't much happening on this side of the sky today. I'm not in school, but Debra and I are both returning in the winter. Sharon is taking a break in solidarity. Every morning, I get up early, sad or not, and make Ari his Bustello. We wake up to smell the coffee, so to speak. And I think of you and your visitation. Even when I'm sad and missing you, I smile when I remember you reprimanding me in that hospital room and know for sure you are still close by. Patty is now my manager at CVS, which is kinda cool. Azizi is still doin' his

thing, recognizing the truth in every situation. Ari has paid for me to get massages every week with a woman named Jessie in Dorchester. I still have bad aching pain from the fall (so to speak). I call her the witch doctor because she says my body is talking to her and she translates it to me. And my body is tellin' me some deep shit. Jessie is the blackest woman I know, blue-black. She receives messages, and as you know, sometimes they're from you. Thanks. This week I want to be a healer. I believe it is the most important job in the world. Jessie and Azizi share their particular brand of specialness. They see beyond. I don't know beyond what. But definitely beyond.

September 29, 2017
Dear S.K.,
This waking up thing is more exciting in a room full of people I love, alive and dead. Staying awake is a whole other story. Truth. There are still times when I can't get out of bed. Is depression a lifelong disease, or is it something you work through little by little, moment by moment? I push myself, mainly for Ari's morning coffee. On my walk to work (walking helps the situation), I work hard at picturing the hospital room, so I can wake up again and again.

Hello, world!

Hello, S.K.!

Then there are mornings like this one that are just plain boring. Nothing happens. Same old, same old. Except for the fact on these mornings, "my fall" plagues me, and I can't forgive myself. How could I hurt everyone like that? Ari says that Rosh Hashanah and Yom Kippur, which is this week, are high holidays because it is about forgiveness, especially forgiving your own damn self. It's also about letting go. I don't get that one at all. I never seem able to let go of anything. Do you know that in the Jewish religion, when someone dies, the family sits Shiva for seven days and tells stories about the family or friend they lost over and over. That makes so much damn sense. I'm thinking of converting to Judaism. Did that ever enter your mind? I think if I could have talked about you, my dad, and my mom more, it would have been good. For my soul that is.

What's really strange is as soon as I wrote this down, my cell rings, and it's Tamika wanting to take me out to lunch, in Jamaica Plain no less. So let's get this straight. Tamika has never taken me out to lunch. I don't think she ever set foot in JP. This should be a trip and a half.

September 30, 2017
The Lunch
Okay. Setting the scene ... again. Tamika picks me up at CVS. When she sees Patty, she gives her a lengthy hug like they are long-lost friends or something. She tries to do the same with Azizi. He moves away and tells her, "No hugs for Azizi." She looks at me, and I let her know by raising my shoulders that it's okay. She smiles at him and says that it's nice to see him. He giggles. Always a good sign for Azizi.

Tamika wants to take me to a nice restaurant, so I suggest J.P. Seafoods, which is nice enough. When we get the menu, she looks a little confused, so I suggest we order the salmon lunch boxes. Things are kinda quiet between us, a little awkward in the beginning. Remember, this is a first. Then, out of nowhere, she just starts talking. It's as if she was reading my mind from yesterday. How could that be? I'm quoting her, but like Patty's birthday speech, it's close but not exact.

"You know, I knew your mom way before I even met your dad."

I was flabbergasted. There was silence. And then I blurted out, "What was she like?"

"She was adventurous, a rebel, a little like you."

I was about to object but stopped myself. Another thought immediately came into my head. It was, *Maybe, just maybe, I am ...* And you were the beginning of my risky spirit.

Then, as if Tamika was reading my mind ... again, she said, "Your friendship with S.K. reminded me of my friendship with her. I was a little jealous of the two of you. I wanted to have a friendship like that again. Michelle and I met like the two of you in high school. She was a grade above me. One day I was being bullied in the lunchroom, and she came to my defense. I was an awkward teen.

She wasn't. Don't know why she did that or what she saw in me, but after that, Michelle took me under her wing. We'd cut school together, get high in the bathroom, shoplift what we needed, hang out in the movies and in our rooms, listening and dancing to music after school. Michelle was a great dancer. She introduced me to her friends. I had a definite crush on her. She was wild but smart and kind of sophisticated. When she went off to college, we lost touch. I was always a little out of her league. I found out later she met your dad in college. I don't know when she started doing the heavy drugs."

I couldn't open my mouth. She continued.

"I met your dad at Slades, a year after she passed. I had no idea he was married to Michelle. He was fine, and I remember building up my nerve and asking him to dance. You know what it feels like when you dance with someone and your bodies are immediately in sync ..."

I didn't, because as you well know, this black girl can't dance, but I nodded my head anyway.

Tamika continued. "I mean, I was ready to screw him right then and there."

TMI.

"But he asked for my number and said he had to go home to his little girl. It's just him and her now. Well, that did it. Hot or not, I was not getting involved with someone who had a daughter. I wasn't ready to be anybody's mother ... But when he called, I couldn't say no. It was that voice, soft and low and sexy and, at the same time, honest. A rare breed. We went out, I must say, to a very nice restaurant, and he began talking about his wife. When he called her Michelle, I almost shit a brick. And when we realized we were in love with the same woman, both of us knew we were meant to be. But the clincher for me was witnessing him with you. How he played with you. How you delighted him. I don't remember ever experiencing family like that, and I knew I wanted to be a part of it."

We both started to weep, right there in the middle of J.P. Seafood. I grabbed my stepmother's hands on the table and held them tight. Though we didn't say the words, we did the Yom Kippur thing. We forgave ourselves and each other.

October

October 1, 2017
I always told you there was more to Tamika than meets the eye. She might have been crude at times and dressed as if she was still living in the early seventies, but she always had real soul. And the greatest polka-dot miniskirt ever made.
MUM ... S.K.

October 1, 2017
Dear Diary,
Again, I got this image of S.K. in the alley with his skirt hiked up, and I wanted to die. I wanted to be with him. I wanted to protect him. I wanted to kill clown forty-five, who stirred up all this hate that fostered S.K.'s rape the day after *that bastard* was elected. I want to kill all those motherfuckers. How could I let this happen to my best friend? I'm a fuckin' wimp. I just don't want to live in a world that promotes hate, racism, homophobia, and ignorance. I just don't.

October 12, 2017
Dear, dear S.K.,
Sorry I haven't written for a few days. Well, actually, over a week. It's been a rough one. Had trouble getting out of bed. Missed a few days of work. Thank God Patty is my supervisor. Just don't know why I get this way. Or maybe I do. I do, and I don't. Anyway, your lover Ari is a saint. Just sayin'. I don't how he puts up with me. Truth. He got

me out of bed and over to Jessie's for a session. So what happened was that my body was talking to her again. Crazy, huh? Well, it wasn't my body. It was you. You were sayin' all kinds of shit to her. Not shit really. It was kind of cool in a way. 'Cause now I have several means of communication with you. She really believes in your presence. Sometimes more than me. And I heard what you said. I mean I really heard it. I'll repeat it again just so you know. You said, or rather she said you said, that I have to call the fall by its real name, attempted suicide. And I have to call your molestation murder. Because the sooner I can name them, the sooner I can heal. And then she made me do it. But I was too hysterical.

And as I'm writing to you now, I don't freakin' feel better. How do I feel? Amazingly sad, like my guts were removed from my body. Like I lost a part of myself and it will never, never return. And at the same time lighter. Able to finally write to you. Strange, huh?

I wanted to say that I miss you more than ever and thank you.

October 13, 2017
You are my twin. I'm feelin' you and listening, babe.
S.K.

October 16, 2017
Hi S.K.,
How are things? Things on this side of the sky are picking up a bit. Last Saturday, Sharon called me. She wanted me to go to a demonstration/march for the dreamers. You know that the shithead and his crew want to take away their rights and send those who have lived here all their lives, earn wages, pay taxes, go to college, back to their original countries. Sick dudes. Truth. She said it might be small, but we need to make our presence felt. They're doing so many nasty things in the name of greed. They don't care about gays or people of color, or the environment, or opiates, or women, or health care, or guns, or Puerto Rico or anything. How could this happen? I hold him directly responsible for your death. That's it. So, I'm going.

Well, this so-called small march had thousands, and I mean thousands, of people. It was last minute, and still … it was an amazing feeling. Like, not only are you not alone in the world, but there are fighters in the trenches, and we're going to do all we can do together. There was so much damn love in this crowd. It made me glad to be alive. Sharon surprised me and brought Debra. And I got Patty, Azizi, and Ari motivated. We were a real live group. I was proud of us. I carried a sign with an enlarged photo of you in Tamika's polka-dotted skirt. So you were definitely making your presence known.

It was organized by Black Lives Matter. And a bunch of them were on a truck, chanting and motivatin' the shit out of all these thousands of people. *So* cool. Sharon wanted to march near the truck, of course. Then she jumped on top. Crazy. But that's Sharon. I could see you up there joining her. Suddenly, I noticed this guy … Remember the guy I followed into the barbershop on my birthday? Well him, next to her on the truck. Sharon was waving to me to come on top, but that was a bit showy for me. Surprisingly, this dude also was waving to me. What the hell? Like he knew me or something. Like he knew I was stalking him that day. I pretended like I didn't see him. Gave him the coldest shoulder. When Sharon came down from the truck, she asked me what the hell that was all about. I said that I didn't know, but she knew otherwise. "When a handsome man waves to you, girl, you wave back. Sometimes I forget you are only eighteen years old."

It's true. I'm such a damn baby.

MUM, especially today …

Nadie

October 17, 2017

Dear Nadie,

What the fuck are you afraid of? And thanks for taking me to the demo …

S.K.

October 18, 2017

Dear S.K.,

Don't know for sure, and you're welcome. Isn't it interesting that there even has to be a movement called Black Lives Matter. That the Trumpettes are upset that black lives matter. That we have to declare that black lives matter so many years after the civil rights movement. That police go on paid leave after they kill a black man, woman, or child. That no one has found your murderers. That just declaring black lives matter is revolutionary. What? And the moron forty-five thinks there are some Nazis who are fine people. Just sayin'. Damn!

October 18, 2017

Nadie, it fuckin' sucks.

S.K.

October 20, 2017

Afternoon, S.K.,

Another boring day. The thing is that I know this sounds weird, but I'm really getting to appreciate these days. I made Ari Bustello before work. The whole kitchen tasted of coffee even before we drank it. We actually had time for conversation, which was pretty ordinary. You know, what's your day look like, the weather, different scenarios in the murder of Trump. Today in Ari's scene, a white man with a striped American flag bandana and the swastika on his back killed poor Ivanka. He went nuts with his AKA rifle. Before he blasted her with bullets, he screamed, "Kill the Jew!" Sad. All perfect and beautiful and blonde and bloody in her cheaply made-out-of-America, original white dress. The news was riddled with stories about devastated Donald. How he cried for his beautiful, perfect daughter, the only woman in his life. What a good girl she was and how devoted she was to all his policies. What kind of person kills the innocent? How he couldn't understand this kind of violence happening in his America. A short, impassioned, tearful speech condemning American Nazis and blaming the fake media. There were going to be huge changes, *huge*. The media was held accountable. That same day, the Republican Party and Congress were right on top of gun control and anti-Semitism. I suppose that is, for once, a *huge* change.

Ari and I make up one every time we feel sad or terrified or helpless or oppressed. That's every morning before we leave the house.

Nothing exciting happened on my walk to CVS this morning. However, it was one of those cool, sunny, windy mornings where I felt your touch on my face while being cocooned in my hooded sweatshirt. Instead of looking down, I remembered to gaze up at the sky, which was baby blue and vast and open. I could get a sense of us, and I felt my lips part in a grin for no obvious reason. I passed all the JP stores as they opened up to the day, and it was as if my body was a magic wand that unlocked each store on the walk. I passed a wild woman with mismatched clothes who sits outside the bank every day hawking *Spare Change*. We see each other a few times a week, and I bought her the usual cup of coffee from DD's and purchased a paper from her for a buck. She always gives me a toothless grin and a "God bless you" that renders me giddy and honored at the same time.

CVS is CVS. Not the most fascinating job in the world. But I'm greeted by Patty and Assisi with good mornings and hugs. I mean, I work with two of my best friends, for heaven's sake.

So, I don't know exactly what I'm saying here. Except, when you think things are boring, same old, same old, it gives you a chance. A chance to peek into the little moments that make life beautiful and kinda special. You're the one who reminded me of that at the foot of my hospital bed. I bow to you, my brother.

October 22, 2017

So, Nadie, my twin, have you heard the latest? Girl, this is a juicy one. Just happened this morning. Will be all over the media. One good thing about being up here is that I have a special front-row seat to everything. But even up here, I was in shock. Nobody knew exactly what happened. The White House aides and staff were running all over the place like chickens without heads. Weird image for me, but that's how I saw it. I'm peering into it now. OMG. I can't believe what I'm witnessing. Blood all over. Who's bleeding? Shit! It's number forty-five and his trusty but oh so scary Kellyanne. Damn. Let me zoom in closer. Kellyanne's face is splattered with blood as well as her blue and white and now red suit. She is yelling at the top of her lungs. Military is dragging her away, kicking and screaming. She's lost it. Totally bonkers. Let me backtrack. What the hell happened? What's that I hear?

"You goddamn motherfuckin' bastard! I've lied every day, developed ulcers, ruined my relationship with my husband, embarrassed my kids, perjured myself, sucked your tiny dick, made up fake news, and now, you heartless bastard, you're firing me. You can't fire me! I know things. I know about the $33 million debt you never intended to pay Puerto Rico after your fuckin' golf course flopped. I know about that thirteen-year-old girl you molested and the real stories about the other twelve women who have come forward. I know about the Russian trollers and how you got elected. I was there; I helped them. I know about each and every one of those four thousand lawsuits against you. I'm telling all, you hear me ... all, and ... I'll kill you, I'll kill you!"

She pulled out a large bowie knife from her red, white, and blue polka-dot Gucci bag. It was so huge at first I thought it was a machete. And damn if she didn't stab him, baby girl. Several times. One was right in the heart. I could almost hear the music from that old *Psycho* movie. But wait a friggin' minute. He should be dead. What the hell is happening? Damn, if we didn't suspect the truth all along, even his dumb-ass base. He just pulled the knife from his heart. Just pulled it right out. Shit ... number forty-five doesn't have a heart. The bastard's alive ... alive!
S.K.

October 22, 2017
Good one. Made my morning. Must tell Ari after work.
Yours,
Nadie

October 24, 2017

My Dear One,

Well, I had a little bit of a shakeup in my ordinary life. Don't know if it's a good or bad shakeup. Didn't look so good. Time will tell. Time … such an interesting phenomena. It changes. So do we. And it never changes; neither do we. One day we're all grown-up, and most days we're that same child we always were. It's hard to get a grip on the paradox. My vocab is improving, don't you think? Must be all the books I'm reading. Speaking of books. I have a new story to tell. It's like the old stories and yet … completely unique. It's us and definitely not us.

All this buildup and mystery to tell a simple tale about a day off, a walk down Centre Street, and an afternoon of stalking. Yes, I said it and did it again. It's like playing detective in real life. I thought it would be like you and me, babe, and how we began. But it was a striking realization that nothing could be like you and me and how we began.

Anyway, I'm walking down Centre, just wandering from my side of town toward JP center. And I see about a half a block in front of me the back of the boy from the barbershop who waved at me from the Black Lives Matter truck. Nobody I know these days here in JP has that particular fade with a touch of blonde on top. I'm curious but keep my distance. Getting good at this. He is taking his good old sweet time too. It's like we're on a stroll together but not together. Anyway, I see him turn down Green Street, so I wait at the corner for a few moments before I turn. Then, to my shock, he goes into that horrible bookstore with the racist owner. What the fuck! However, I'm fascinated he chooses a bookstore, especially that one. When he is definitely inside, I walk up to the door. I build up my nerve, which takes a few minutes of idling in front, and walk in. After all, bookstores are my thing too. Well, apparently the bitch has taken over three stores, knocked down the walls, so it's a café and bookstore. I have to admit, it's kinda dope. The walls are golds and burnt oranges and purples. But I'm still very, very skeptical because of that weird interaction I had before with the owner. I guess people and bookstores can change, but …

I sit down and look at the small menu. Who comes to the table as a waiter but the barbershop dude. He smiles. It's beautiful and warm, and he has surprisingly white teeth. I order a muffin and American coffee. He lingers for some reason, which gives me enough time to build up my nerve.

I stutter. "How l-long have you worked here?"

"Oh, about a month," he answers.

He returns with my muffin and coffee.

So then I ask the million-dollar question. "Do you like the owner?"

"I love her," he says with a shit-eatin' grin on his face.

Damn, he's sleeping with that sleazy bitch. I take a humongous bite of my muffin to stuff down I don't know what and begin to choke. Barbershop guy taps my back, and pieces of banana muffin go flying across the room. So fuckin' embarrassing. He just stares and laughs. In fact, the whole damn café is giggling. I'm devastated and can't speak. Finally, Barbershop asks if I'm okay.

"Fine," I stammer. "Just took too big of a bite." Well, there goes crap for not bringing attention to myself.

When he returns later with the check, he has the nerve to question me. "Do I know you?"

"No," I respond with just a note of bitterness I can't control, pay the check, and haul ass out the door.

As you can imagine, that didn't go as planned. However, I had to ask myself, what the hell did I plan?

October 25, 2017
Nadie, did you ever have a plan? Don't obsess. Let it go. You know you need to.
MUM,
S.K.

October 31, 2017—Halloween
Dear S.K.,
You know me all too well. Ari told me I had to stop talking about Barbershop and his bitch of a girlfriend because I was driving him

nuts. So, I devised a plan. That's right, a plan. When I told Ari and let him know, not only was he included but he will be the star, he clapped his hands in excitement. At that moment, I realized he loved theatre as much as you.

We plotted out our scene. I would be returning to the bookstore with my handsome, older, Harvard-grad white boyfriend. He liked that but had many questions. What should we wear? How should we style our hair? How about hats? How intimate should we be? How long should we wait before the return? We went with hipsterish, fake tattoos, all black, a funky Pharrell hat for him, a shocking patch of blue in my hair, no kissing but lots of eye gazing, handholding, whispering, and giggling, and Halloween.

We located a semiprivate table in the corner, almost surrounded by bookshelves. If I were coming here alone, this would be my table. I have to give girlfriend creds. It was a dream bookstore/café. As Ari glanced around the café, I recognized that he appreciated this little spot also. I nonchalantly scanned our surroundings and saw no sign of Barbershop, just some old, gray-haired white lady serving coffee to the customers and chatting everyone up.

When she spotted us, she called to someone in the back room, and Barbershop comes running out to wait on us. Oddly enough, the room just wasn't that crowded and certainly didn't warrant another waiter on the floor. I squeezed Ari's hand under the table. And with an extra smile, giggle, and eye locking, our Halloween theatre piece began.

Our acting technique was superb. Maybe I'll become an actress. I do have some talent in that department. It would be great to be different people and step out of my own character every now and then. I certainly need an escape. Sometimes I'm just too much for my own damn self.

Ari and I were so gooey; it was hard to resist breaking into raucous laughter. We were totally engrossed in our roles and really almost did miss Barbershop standing in front of us ready to take our order. When I managed to tear away from Ari and look up, Barbershop questioned with a definite edge, "Do you want to order or should I come back?"

I squinted toward him, almost batting my eyelashes, and replied, "Sorry. We were celebrating Ari's graduation from Harvard." I really wanted to get that in. We just ordered coffee. I didn't want to risk another banana muffin. He delivered the check by slapping, and I mean slapping, it on the table. Ari whispered in my ear, still in character, "I do believe Barbershop is jealous."

When we exited, Ari was hyper-enthused at our performance and yacked on about it during our entire walk home. I, on the other hand, had a queasy sensation in the pit in my stomach that I couldn't shake.

November

November 1, 2017
Right. Of course you did because you're an asshole.
S.K.

November 3, 2017
You're right. You are always right. I hate you! That's what I get for trying to plan my life, damn it. Life isn't a scene or a skit. There are things I can't control. Damn it to hell. Retaliation isn't the fuckin' answer. Though I do wish I could murder the motherfuckers who molested and killed you. Slow, painful deaths. But, Barbershop, he was just being nice. Maybe girlfriend didn't show him the side she showed me. Not yet anyway. And what's it my business anyhow. Sharon's right. I'm still such a baby. So, I'm going back to the café. To come clean. Just have to build up my nerve.
Nadie

November 6, 2017
So, I decided to keep you abreast of current events. I mean, you probably are but just in case. Had a long conversation with Debra, my mentor and teacher and all-around fantastic person. We were so excited that finally Mueller and his team have issued indictments of several of Trump's people in his campaign and in his cabinet. Debra says that this is how it began before Nixon resigned. It's so cool to know someone who lived during that time and could give me

firsthand information. It may mean impeachment; it may not. But for right now, this is all we have. And it uplifts my spirits. When I remember the picture of you forever embedded in my brain the day after forty-five got elected, with a swastika and a Trump button on your chest, I'm beyond heartbroken. I'm beyond angry. I'm beyond devastated. So, this is for you, for now, and for all of us who are suffering.

MUM ... Nadie

November 8, 2017

Well, well, well ... do I have a story to tell you. I'm gonna take my good old sweet time with this one, so you can appreciate all the nuances. Like that word? I'm becoming quite the wordsmith. So, I did it. I went back to the café/bookstore. But I admit, Ari got me baked beforehand. I had to walk around the block several times just to come down. And when my head felt slightly buzzed but empty of chatter, I nonchalantly (I think) walked in. My now-favorite table was empty; someone just left as I walked in. The cup and saucer and his book weren't even cleared yet. I swear it felt as if this guy at my table left for me to take it. He looked at me when I walked in the door, smiled, and immediately vacated the premises. I think this is less paranoia and more a dance. Just sayin'.

Barbershop sauntered over to clear the table and apologized for the delay. There really was no delay. I told him that the last customer exited so quickly he left his book. Barbershop laughed. There were those pearly white teeth. Beautiful. Strange that a guy can be beautiful. Except for you of course. But you were always the exception. He proceeded to tell me it was part of the ambience of the café. He used that word ... that a book was left for anyone to take home or read in the hopes the person who picked it up also left a book.

"How the heck does the bookstore make money?" I asked.

He smiled again and told me it's a choice to buy or trade. And money was made.

For a quick second, I thought about bringing *Sula* back but knew I just couldn't part with it ... yet.

When I asked if this was the brainstorm of the owner, he nodded yes and said he would be right back to take my order. Damn, this is the brainstorm of the same woman whose condescending eyes followed me around the store and belligerently answered my questions. I couldn't believe it. But as Patty would say, shit changes. Look at Patty.

When he returned, I ordered a cappuccino, my new favorite drink. He followed up by asking me if I wanted to brave a banana muffin. We both laughed. So good to be able to laugh at myself. I was able to tell him yes. Then I gathered all my nerve to ask him if the owner was his girlfriend.

He laughed again. He is the *laughiest* guy. "No," he responded between guffaws. I really didn't know what was so funny. However, this was the closest to a conversation I ever had with him, so I wanted to keep it going.

"Well," I added, "you did tell me you love her."

"Yes," Barbershop replied, "I do see how you would get that impression." Then, he continued, "Is Harvard your boyfriend?"

I didn't laugh, but I didn't exactly come completely clean. "Oh no, he's just my roommate. We're very close and were celebrating his graduation."

"So you said." A little edge there. I kinda liked the edge, as much as the laugh, but not as much as the smile.

"Enjoy the coffee and especially the muffin. But if you need the Heimlich, I'm right behind the counter." I laughed, a little stupid, embarrassing, hiccup-type giggle, and he left me to my own devices.

The book was still on the café table. I think you know the title of that book. I wondered, was it left on purpose by the guy who suddenly rose when I entered? Did you and he leave this for me? I remember him smiling at me and carefully placing it on the table.

I sipped my coffee, feeling the mustache of whipped milk pleasantly lining my upper lip, slowly ate my banana muffin, and picked up the novel in front of me. I started to read:

> It was the best of times, it was the worst of times, it
> was the age of wisdom, it was the edge of foolishness,

it was the epoch of belief, it was the epoch of incredulity, it was the season of light, it was the season of darkness, it was the spring of hope, it was the winter of despair, we had everything before us, we had nothing before us …

"Damn!" I exclaimed, a little too loud for comfort. Others turned toward me and then went back to their diaries, devices, books, coffee. The older waitress laughed. Barbershop came over.

"Sorry," I whispered.

"Oh no, don't be sorry. Never be sorry."

He sat down … at my table, no less. *Shit,* I didn't say out loud.

"You know that was written in a magazine in installments from April 30 to November 26 in 1859."

"Damn," I said again. A tower of knowledge, that Barbershop.

"For real," he replied.

"How could some guy in 1859 write my heart?"

"I know, right? That's how I felt. The novel was one of several motivations to be an activist. Well, the novel, Malcolm X, Angela Davis, and the damn murders of black men by our so-called police force."

"You mean your involvement in Black Lives Matter."

"So you did see me wave to you."

"Yeah, I'm an asshole sometimes."

"I think you're pretty cool." As he got up from his seat across from me, he looked me right in the eye. "Nice meeting you …" and waited.

"Nadine." What could I do but volunteer (sort of) my name?

He held my hand. Very gallant of him. And with a nod, pretty close to a wink, "Dewayne, Dewayne Carter," he revealed.

Barbershop was Dewayne. I'll miss Barbershop. But I like Dewayne. And I'm in love with Charles. Dickens, that is.

At first, I thought I had overstayed my welcome, which made me embarrassed. But when I searched the premises, I noticed there were customers who were at the café longer than me. We were a small but odd group. A skinny, pale white guy with oily hair and horn-rimmed glasses, an older woman with a large green velvet hat, and a hip young interracial couple, both with dreads and shaved sides. In a strange but natural way, I was a fit. It was a place for the out-of-place. I felt so grown-up in this café. I was absorbed in the world of *A Tale of Two Cities*, the world of the café, my thoughts and my dreams, all at the same time. I felt … what was the word for it … happy. I had come closer than I would like to think to never experiencing this flirtation with Barbershop, this time in and out of myself. Fuck, I almost ended my life. I'm not sayin' I still don't feel the ache of the reality that I left you alone when I knew something was not right or the loss I often feel about you, my mom and dad, or the anger that wells up at the oddest times, or fits of tears for no reason whatsoever, or those moments when I just can't get out of bed. But the absolute fact of the matter is that a *you* in my life brought me more joy than you can even imagine. I became my whole self because of you. We stretched each other. We were brother and sister in another life. What the hell, in this life. For the first time in a long while, I began seeing images, like watching a movie inside my brain, of us … getting baked in the school bathroom, in my bedroom, at the back lot of The Strand, walking to Upman's Corner, holding hands, in our miniskirts, singing our version of Beyonce's "Single Ladies," dancing like crazy in gym at Dot High when nobody was there, dreaming our futures, trying on Tamika's wigs and parading the hood with them on, laughing till we peed … Suddenly in the middle of my reverie, I noticed Dewayne standing in front of my table.

"Wow," he said. "I've been standing here for over a minute. You really entered another world."

"Did I?" I muttered.

He gave me the check and then surprised me. "My d-dog is out back," he stuttered. I didn't notice a stutter before. The guy was actually nervous, maybe as nervous as me. "We're going for a long walk. Y-you could join me?"

"Sure," I answered, trying to be nonchalant about the whole thing. And then added, "I love dogs."

Do I?

Walking the Dog

This is what it was like walking with Dewayne and his dog. Silence. Pure. Fresh silence. Magical silence. From the moment we left the café, whether his dog led us through the busy streets of JP, or back roads, or Franklin Park, the two of them introduced me to a quiet I had never known. His dog knew his way to no way. It was clear that Dewayne and I were in capable paws. And every now and then, injected into the silence was conversation. Conversation that bubbled up and circled and brought up memories or heartfelt ideas. Not unlike our conversations, my dear S.K. It might have missed some of our flamboyance together but not that high of stoned timelessness (as if we were on some really good shit). Like now was stretching till forever. The walk and talk reminded me of us and how you are a still voice, a wildness, a friendship that has never left me.

Dewayne, his dog, and I must have walked for hours because the light changed toward the end. But I'm jumping forward. And in order to really tell this story, I must stick to the moments, go slow, and picture everything in its time. Or at least, this is what Sharon and Debra tell me.

So, as I said, in the silence, conversation rose and fell at a rhythm neither of us was used to but both of us inherently knew. It was easy. It was honest. It was revealing yet remained so natural I believe neither of us felt exposed.

Dewayne told me that he had a past. That's how he put it. A past—stealing cars, going to detention, dropping out of high school, selling drugs. "I was a fuckin' thug," he announced, with a wistfulness, a sadness in his proclamation. And when a good friend of his needed money for an abortion, he found himself selling crack, something he said he would never do. His dad is an addict in jail, and he lives with his grandmother and aunt (another crack addict).

"Where's your mom?" I asked.

"She just couldn't handle me anymore and moved in with her new man."

There was no anger in his voice, just an acceptance, as if anybody would do that to her son. I thought of Tamika and how difficult I've been and how she never left me or kicked me out. I thought about how she loves me, even though she wasn't my so-called real mother. And how I hated her for so goddamn long. Shit, and I thought I had it rough.

"Obviously something changed. What was it?"

He looked at me and stopped for a second in reflection. Even his dog came to a halt and obediently sat, as if on command. "I was at my lowest," he continued. "My next stop was prison. The idea I was growing into my dad struck me to the core. I don't know what changed me except the fact I just couldn't stand me anymore. I hated my life. I hated what I was becoming. And seriously, I wasn't having fun. Everything was on rote, and I was no longer controlling me. I was a puppet of the system. Well, maybe I didn't have those words yet. But that was the sensation. That was the sick feeling inside."

"I know that feeling," I barely uttered.

"Somehow I knew that. I knew the day you followed me into the barbershop." And again with the smile that could turn anyone into mush.

I could have objected and denied it, but what was the point? After all, it was the damn truth. You know it. I know it. And apparently he knew it. For the first time, I understood the word *swoon*. It was that damn smile.

We began walking again. "It was that barbershop," Dewayne exclaimed. "There are places in life where magic happens."

"I know, like my GED class or the café."

"Exactly. Right. The café ... I must have passed Pablo's Barbershop a million times. After all, it was right down Centre, just a few blocks from the projects. But that day, my lowest day, I walked in. Pablo said that I was in luck. There was no one waiting. A rare thing, I was to find out later. He stared at me in the mirror and laughed. I was ready to leave right there and then. But then he said, 'You need a change.' Truer words were never spoken. Pablo kinda designed my hair. Shaved it on the sides with a part and shaved the greatest design in the back of triangles that were all linked. Like the life I wanted to lead but had no image or words for until that moment. When I left, I smack bumped into the bookshop owner before she owned it and her dog. And there began an unlikely friendship."

I wanted to interject, "You can say that again," but didn't. Instead, unlikely friendship brought about the appearance of motor mouth, and of course, you came to mind and mouth. I told him our story from the beginning. Yes, how I stalked you at first. He laughed. I suppose it's an odd way to begin and then begin again. Dewayne laughed so easily, like he smiled but loud and full and natural, like breathing. But what made it even more than that was what he began with, his struggles in life. What a feat. What courage. The courage to laugh.

I digress. You. You and me. So many of our stories. Like how we had matching polka-dotted skirts borrowed (sort of) from Tamika, who had three of the same in different colors and polka dots. How you danced and I joined you, fearlessly in the streets of Dorchester. The day I confided in you (I had never told anyone) about my mom and dad and their deaths, and you sobbed with me, even more than me, which finally brought about fits of hysterics and runs to the bathroom. How you introduced me to a new life, new people like Ari. And art and jazz and Nina Simone and Chaka Kahn. How I left you, knowing it just wasn't right, and you were murdered that day, the day after the clown came to power with the rise of hatred. I told him about my birthday, Patty and her speech, Ari, Assisi and his talents, Sharon, Debra and breast cancer. Depression. I even told him about my failed attempt at suicide. I couldn't shut up.

After my purge, there was silence again. Just walking. Following his dog's lead. I couldn't tell if I felt relieved or ashamed. Somehow Barbershop (his nickname forever) knew. He grabbed my hand and said as he looked straight ahead, "I'm so glad you failed."

"Yeah," also straight ahead, "failure ain't so bad."

His reply was something you would say, "True d'at."

We continued the walk holding hands. His grip was strong and soft at the same time. I swear his dog kept looking back at us approvingly, or maybe just to make sure we were still there. By the way, this was an animal who knew the streets; you had to love him. It looked like we were on our way to Jamaica Pond, but we went through so many twists and turns I wasn't really sure. And that was okay by me.

Out of the blue but not out of the blue at all, just another twist, Dewayne began talking about his involvement with Black Lives Matter and how it gave his life purpose. A deeper meaning, not denying his past or outside of this past but part of it. Activism was similar and opposite to acting out. It had all of the energy, drive, and some of the consequences but none of the shit and self-hate. His life was no longer just about him but larger, deeper, and connected. There was a power in his life now.

You have to admit, that was kinda cool. He used the phrase "agent of change." I thought, *Whatever I am or become in life, whether it be teacher, reader, writer, or activist, I want to be an agent of change.* I want to do something; I want to say something that honors you, my dad, my mom, Patty, Debra, even Tamika (maybe especially Tamika) that makes our lives, our struggles matter in this crazy world. And I want to do it now.

Barbershop turned to me and stated, "We're living in scary times." Nothing had happened in the moment to frighten either of us. It was just a simple acknowledgment. A crazy truth. "All the good things Obama did are being dismantled," he added.

"It's overwhelming. The rise of hate crimes, the death of S.K. ... Sometimes Ari and I make up little scenarios just to get us out the damn door." I told him the Ivanka and Kellyanne story. His laughter was contagious. Both of us, cracking up and walking. We must have been a sight.

Then Barbershop (the nickname just fits him, even more so now that I know his story) stops in his tracks and turns toward me. "But the real stories are sometimes even freakier. Did you hear about Trump's big fallout with Pence?"

I shook my head no.

"It's all over the internet. The VP has been having not-so-secret meetings with top Republicans mapping out the overthrow of Trump and the replacement of Pence, their version of repeal and replace. They're planning to make another homophobic, racist nut president. Really, it's hard to figure out who's sleazier in that party. Well, Trump was rip shit mad. He charged into Pence's home and practically busted in the door. When he realized the asshole was still in bed, he burst into his bedroom. And lo and behold, Pence was in bed with mother. But her wig was off, and s/he had a full-blown erection! That's right, mother is a man! Trump tweeted like never before, which is a feat in itself."

"What?" I pulled out my phone.

Barbershop broke out in hysterics. I was punked. And I must admit, well done for a spur-of-the-moment punk.

Silence. Walking. I was thinking, *Perhaps this is the beginning of a great friendship, and whatever else comes with it is icing on the cake.* I remembered how you and I talked about joining True Colors OUT Youth Theater when we were still dreaming of change.

I asked Dewayne how he got involved with Black Lives Matter. His answer was direct and to the point. He said that it evolved. I know, right? He used that word. "There was my life and the life of my friends and family, I was changing, and this dog's mom turned me on to writers like Angela Davis and James Baldwin that rocked my world."

"So you never consummated your relationship." God I'm a jealous bitch.

He giggled in his response, "She's old enough to be my grandma."

Then it hit me like ten-pound barbells. Wings Café was magic. Of course, there was a different owner.

In the middle of my discovery, I looked up and noticed the light was changing. Dewayne's semi adopted dog, literally led us into the sunset over Jamaica Pond. The three of us—a delinquent turned agent of change, an eighteen-year-old learning to forgive herself, and three-legged German Shepherd—remained in stillness, mirroring the trees, until we were one with darkness.

Acknowledgements

It takes a community to live a rich, blessed, and sometimes-even charmed life as a woman, lesbian, introvert, retired teacher, and creative artist. It is with profound appreciation that I thank the most amazing, loving family of friends who donated funds to make Lulu possible, inspire me daily, provide laughs and an ear when I need one most, invited me to after dinner readings at their home to hear a work in progress, *audienced* my plays, volunteered as board members and actors of our theatre company back in the day, opened their homes to living room readings of my last book, *God s a Dog,* and bought my book not only for themselves but for their friends. I have known, adored and treasured many on this list for over forty years (one of the perks of getting older). Thank you Ellen Balis and Doug McLeod, Dede Ketover and Nancy Carlucci, Shani Dowd, Judy Pomerantz, Betsy Smith and Berit Pratt, Susan Wilber and Debbie Campbell, Melanie Berzon and Lesley Sternin, Joanne O'Neil, Sharon Howell, Nancy Hughes, Michael Baxter and Sander Kramer, Sharon Locke, Warren and Martha Gabow, Myra Hindus and Jewel Jackson, Jeanette Muzima and Frances Blasque, Debbie Lubarr, Laura Hubbard, Diane Goss, Pam Hall, Amy Mandel, and Paula Gallitano.

Thank you Moish and Tibie Gabow who visit often with Pastrami sandwiches from the neighborhood deli, singing Cole Porter tunes, and giving needed advice in my dreams.

Special thanks to Michelle Baxter who helps me overcome my

cynicism about long-term relationships and teaches me how to love fully and deeply every day.

Thank you to the numerous friends, family, students and teachers, who keep me inspired and educated.

And finally, it with deep appreciation that I thank the small kindnesses of strangers and acquaintances who change my life in subtle but meaningful ways. There are so many of them, but for now I want to thank the sweet, gentle man who sells Spare Change in JP Center with a smile that can transform any mood, while noticing my array of hats with a flair of his own every time I pass, the manicurist who painted my toenails a rainbow of colors as a surprise because she knew she could, and the woman in Boomerangs who had me close my eyes so she could finally show me the wings she purchased that day. They were a few of the prophets who inspired and inhabited characters in this book.